THE HOOK and THE HAYMAKER

Stories by Jared Yates Sexton

Split Lip Press

Published by Split Lip Press
1309 W. Broad Street #307
Richmond, VA 23220
www.splitlippress.com
www.splitlipmagazine.com

ISBN: 978-0-9909035-2-9

Cover design by S. McDaniel

✪ CONTENTS ✪

ACKNOWLEDGEMENTS

Some stories have appeared previously in the following publications: The Hook and The Haymaker in *Buffalo Almanack*, Maggie in *Southern Humanities Review*, Punch-For-Punch in *PANK*, Yankee in *Hobart*, Outlaws in *Joyland Magazine*, It Comes With The Territory in *Pithead Chapel*, Coming Home in *The Account*, Volcano in *Revolution House*, Bear Fight in *Night Train*, That's How A Man Lives in *The Bicycle Review*, Behold, I Come As A Thief in *Split Lip Magazine* and *The Best of the Net Anthology*, Monsieur and Mademoiselle in *NEAT*, Live Off The Land in *Stymie Magazine*, In All Their Squalor in *Inkwell Magazine*, and Need in *Midwestern Gothic*.

THIS BOOK IS FOR

SAM
CLH
BKD
MRM

THE HOOK
✪ AND THE HAYMAKER ✪

YOU MAY NOT believe it, but I fought Buster Mathis before he was Buster Mathis. He was still fighting the City Circuit, after the Golden Gloves and before he moved up in class and dropped Harper Lawrence for the title. They were training him at Patterson's Gym, the place where all the up-and-comers go, and they needed some sparring partners. I signed up and they hired me right off. His manager said I worked hard and didn't take cheap shots. Said he admired the left hook I was throwing back in those days.

Back then Buster went through partners like they were toilet paper. I stood out there on call and watched him drop them one after another. They'd get in and touch gloves and he'd put them on their ass before they knew what was what. He was a murderer. Couldn't even hold back sparring. He'd flick a jab or two and then lay out these poor boys with a cross or uppercut. Just shut their lights right off.

What was worse was his mighty haymaker. That's what he was famous for, this wild punch that started in his right shoulder and came up and over your guard like a flood. Seems like he landed it every time. Certainly put Harper Lawrence down. And when he let loose that day, when he'd square up one of those kids who went ahead of me, it wasn't even a contest. They took it right in the teeth.

They fell and they fell hard.

Truth be told, I wasn't looking forward to getting in the ring. Guy before me had to be carried out. But I climbed in anyway and got a mouthpiece from one of the corners. He told me to try and stay in there awhile and swap punches.

Throw that hook, he said. Make him earn it.

I didn't know any better. Sure, I said.

Buster charged at the bell. Come right in like I didn't mean shit to him. He swiped with his right, that goddamn cannon of his, and it barely got my cheek. It hurt though, cracked a molar, and that was enough to snap me awake. I got the hell away and ducked the jab he was loading up. Out of desperation I hurled that hook, the one that'd got his manager's attention, and it smacked him spot on the ear.

Now, I never did much as a fighter. I won my share and lost just as many. But I'll be honest - that hook of mine had to be one of the best in the business. It had to be. I knew from early on I didn't have much to offer. Feet were slow. Knuckles broke too easy. I couldn't manage a long bout or front a defense to save my life. But that hook? It was my saving grace, the one tool I had in my bag worth a damn.

Well. Buster found out about it. When it hit he backed off, stumbled even, and had to take a second to get his head in order. I could tell it shook him up, that it made him think things over.

His manager was up on the apron. Buster, you good son?

He was looking at me through his worn-out eyes before he nodded and charged again. This time I could feel heat coming off him like exhaust. I didn't see much except that haymaker charging up in his lump of a right shoulder. After it landed it was a good half hour before I came to and I'd swallowed four of my front teeth.

They slipped me some extra scratch for the surgery. I pocketed a couple hundred and told the dentist to only replace three of those teeth. I wanted a memento. Now, when I smile, people get a good look at the souvenir I got from Buster Mathis.

Things changed after that. Word spread that I'd stood the man up. I got more fights, even got a shot at the City Champion. Fought that Hector Ramos guy at the Roosevelt Gym and got knocked out in the seventh. There was word that Ramos was dirty and put pig iron in his gloves. But I didn't protest. I was finished fighting at that point, done waking up with bloody sheets and bruised hands. I'd done my time.

Of course, Buster was just taking off. Got on a real roll of it and was taking fellas out left and right. I used to go to the bar to drink and watch. Sometimes people would come up and ask if I was the guy who'd stood Buster Mathis with a left hook. They'd want autographs and pictures like I was some kind of big shot. It was embarrassing, but I'd grin my big gap-toothed smile and bear it.

The paper even called later and did a story in the run-up to his fight with Harper Lawrence. This pretty little reporter came and asked what it was like to take a punch from Buster Mathis and live. I laughed and pointed to where my tooth had been. Like falling, I said.

Her name was Anne and she was sweet enough to laugh at my piss-poor joke. In fact, she laughed at all my piss-poor jokes. She was fifteen years younger but I could tell she'd spent most of her life in the company of her elders. I asked if she wanted to grab a bite to eat and the two of us went over to the Mexican joint down the street. We closed the place down, drinking cervezas and going over all my old, worthless fights. When the article finally ran in the paper it was crammed way in the back.

It wasn't two weeks later Anne moved in. When we'd met she'd been in a bad situation and looking for a way out. I guess I gave her that. And maybe it was out of appreciation, or even kindness, but we spent most of our nights getting drunk on the couch and watching fights on the tube. In those days you could count on somebody airing a bout, be it cruisers or feathers or the occasional heavy, and we'd be right there when the opening bell rang, the both of us draining beers between her asking questions and me doing my best to explain.

When it came to the technical aspects of the sport, the poetics she called it, I hardly knew anything. As a fighter I was clumsy, a cloud of mistimed punches and artless blocks, and the fact that I'd ever won a decision

—

or knocked a man out was a miracle in and of itself, but all I wanted was to impress her so I faked it. Look there, I'd say to her, pretending to know what I was talking about. Look how he drops that guard. Look at that window.

I see it, she'd say and huddle in close.

She was as sweet of a thing as I'd ever come across. In the morning she'd head into the office to report on a car crash or an assault and of the evening she'd come and make me supper. Never asked me to find work. Never bothered me about my drinking. Never asked me to do anything besides explain the fights on the television.

Well, she asked one thing.

After Buster Mathis retired he came back to the city. Put his name on a drive-in that lasted two seasons and shut down in good order. Bankrolled a diner that burned up under suspicious circumstances. I'd see him every now and then walking in and out of places. You could tell he was enjoying retirement. A layer of fat coated his muscles and his face and cheeks filled out. But just watching him you could tell he was still graceful, one of the most naturally gifted sons of bitches to ever lace up the gloves.

And he was as famous as they came round here. Every time somebody opened a store or restaurant they'd ask Buster to come and cut the ribbon or declare business begun. He seemed bored by the whole thing. Like he was half-asleep when he got out there. He'd put up those cinderblock fists of his like he was about to fight for the photographs, but the spirit was gone.

One of those openings was for the new Shop N Save

on Bondehoo. There was going to be some sort of big ceremony, the kind he was always brought in for, and over beers Anne said she thought I should be there too.

I'll write it up, she said, for the paper. Get a picture and everything.

Nobody cares, I said back. And there's no way Buster would even remember me.

She didn't agree. This is the kind of thing people eat up, she said. Hell, it might be on the front page. You never know, maybe they'll start asking you to open up supermarkets.

Before I would've told her no, straight up, but something had changed. It was as if something had shut off, like we were both tired and ready to throw in the towel. We got hateful there for a while and sometimes I'd ask her about it and she'd act like I was imagining the whole thing. It was there though and I knew I wasn't in a position to turn her down. After all, a girl like her, a girl who can put up with a washed-up loser like me for so long, doesn't ask for much. But when they do, it matters.

So I said okay.

The morning of she helped me put on the only suit I owned. It wouldn't button anymore and the shirt only made it halfway up my chest. The whole deal just reminded me just how out of shape I was. And, when I went to button the buttons that would still cooperate, my knuckles started feeling fuzzy and out of focus. A pain throbbed up. It's how they felt whenever there was a rain brewing, whenever they remembered the old days between the ropes.

I don't know if I can do this, I said.

6

She tied a loose knot in my tie and brought her face close to mine. I know you can, she said. You can do anything you want to do, she said.

I wish I could've told her how wrong she was.

At the new supermarket there were maybe thirty people there in front of the main stage. Some reporters, a television crew from the news station, the store employees, and a few gawkers and family members. Over the top of the stage was a banner - SHOP N SAVE: THE UNDISPUTED GROCERY CHAMPION. Next to the words was a pair of badly drawn boxing gloves.

When the time came the owner marched out with the new managers. Some music played. I can't remember what it was. The air was buzzing around my ears. I was keeping watch for Buster while Anne was squeezing my hand in anticipation. I wanted to run.

And now, the owner said, pulling a cheap-looking championship belt out of a box, the meanest man to ever throw a punch – Buster Mathis.

More music played. A few purple spots danced in front of my eyes. I tongued the space between my teeth. Buster came onstage and the crowd barely cheered while he made a show of throwing a few punches. I felt my feet shift on their own and had to catch myself from falling over.

Buster got up to the microphone and the owner tried to drape the championship belt on his shoulder. It was awkward but it ended up there like a dead snake. Buster said something but the microphone was turned off. He backed away and the owner announced he'd sign some autographs if anybody wanted them.

He ended up behind a table on the stage. The

7

reporters and employees and gawkers went from getting some of the free food to getting autographs from Buster. Anne led me up there in line and got her photographer ready.

You're shaking, she whispered to me.

I'm not shaking, I lied.

I got up to Buster and he was signing a receipt slip for a teenager wearing a Shop N Save polo. Chances were he didn't even know who Buster was. Soon as he got the autograph he shoved the slip into his pocket and walked off to find something to drink. He'd had no idea how great Buster was, how he'd gone round the world knocking some of the biggest and the strongest on their asses. It was awful.

Next, said the man directing traffic.

I walked up and said, Hey, Buster. It wasn't much more than a whisper.

Buster wasn't paying attention. He'd signed his name for the people before me with his head down, like he was ashamed of what he'd become or that he'd had to be there in the first place. I imagine he was probably thinking back to his days of being led out to the ring, crowds of people cheering and the music pumping out of the speakers. I'd bet every last cent I had he was wishing he was anywhere but this sad-ass city that'd birthed him.

Buster, Anne said to him. I'm from the paper. You remember this fella? You remember sparring back in the day?

Like waking from a nap, Buster lazily raised his head. He looked like someone who might have been Buster Mathis in a previous life. Like someone who missed being Buster Mathis. Then those eyes of his, the same I'd seen after I landed that cross, the tired and worn-out ones, they came to me. I can't even begin to tell you why, but I think he recognized me right off.

I'd like to do a story, Anne said to him. A sort of a where-are-they-now piece.

I don't think she was done speaking at that point but she quit talking. Buster, after all, was lifting himself out of his seat. He was raising that mountain of a body of his up and shedding the suit coat that barely fit him. Those eyes came alive too. They caught fire like someone had switched on an engine.

Buster, I said.

But I'd been watching his eyes too closely. It was a flaw of mine from way back, one of the things that'd always got me in hot water in the late rounds. I'd be in there in the mix and get to focusing on the fella's eyes instead of where it needed to be——his feet and his hands. And right then, on the stage, Anne at my side, I was watching how Buster's moved and changed and not paying a bit of mind to where all the trouble was brewing and swelling, there in that right shoulder.

✪ MAGGIE ✪

MAGGIE WAS A WIDOW of seven years and every Sunday her husband's brother Dick dropped in to keep her company and play cards. She would fix a pot of spaghetti, Dick's favorite, while he drank beer and told her about his week. He worked at the same mine where his brother had been killed, so he was careful with the details.

After a few plates they would clean the table and put the dishes in to soak. Then Dick would open a few more bottles of beer and the two of them would play rummy. Maggie took her time looking for runs while Dick talked and let her win. As it got late she would fold her hand and tell him she was ready for bed. They would say goodbye and Dick would leave with the beer they hadn't drank.

When he arrived one Sunday he found Maggie cooking chili and pacing about the kitchen, pulling spices from the shelf above the stove and emptying canned tomatoes into the pot. She looked pretty and more alive than he'd seen her in awhile. Without a word he sat at the table and opened a beer for himself.

I forgot, she said, shaking some salt into the soup. I went to the store today and I forgot.

What? Dick said. He took a drink and leaned forward. What was that?

I went to the store today, she said, like I do every Sunday. I went in there and I meant to pick up some tomatoes and pasta for your dinner. I had a list with me and everything.

Lists are good, Dick said. I use lists all the time. Very forgetful.

And I pushed my cart, aisle to aisle, she said. She took a long wooden spoon from a drawer and stirred the pot. And I watched myself do it. Watched myself grab the beans and the peppers. I knew what I was doing.

Of course you did, Dick said. He settled back then and had himself a drink. You wanted a change. Change isn't so bad.

Steam was rising from the pot then and she took a potholder and waved it off. I went in the back and grabbed the whiskey, she said. Even made sure it was the right kind.

Dick looked over the table and saw the bottle. He finished his beer and grabbed a small glass from the cabinet and made himself a whiskey with a splash of water. It's very good, he said. Probably my favorite.

And then I almost got into the checkout when I remembered, she said. I thought to myself, he likes a little bit of cheese on top. Just a little sprinkling of cheese.

11

Dick sipped his whiskey and water and nodded. You know me, he said.

Maggie didn't speak much then and focused on the cooking while Dick drank and told her some stories about the mine. When the chili was finished she ladled a bowl for him and watched while he ate.

It wasn't until they'd loaded the sink that she said, Isn't that crazy?

Isn't what crazy? Dick said, scraping his bowl with a pad.

To do something like that, she said.

Like what? he said. Like wanting something different for a change? People do it every day. He was done with his bowl then and was holding his whiskey and water in one hand and had the other on the small of Maggie's back.

Making up someone's favorite meal like that, she said. Going to all that trouble and all.

Wait, Dick said.

Going into a store and buying the fixings, she said. Cooking all day for someone who isn't gonna walk through the door.

Dick put his whiskey and water down and looked at her.

I forgot he was gone, Maggie said. How does something like that happen?

He said he didn't know and helped her finish scrubbing the pots and pans.

Afterwards he dealt a couple of hands of rummy but could tell Maggie wasn't interested as she held her cards so loosely they slipped out of her fingers and onto the table. No matter how hard he tried to lose, Dick won every time. He was about to deal again when the phone rang. It was his mother, Maggie's mother-in-law.

Maggie left her cards behind and walked into the other room with the phone. She was loud enough that Dick could hear talking about the chili and his brother. He slapped his cards on the table and took his drink into the living room, where he couldn't hear anymore.

The house hadn't changed in years. Every last thing was still in its place, as if it were stuck in time. His brother's recliner stayed put next to the television and all of the magazines in the rack were the same ones he'd been reading the night before the accident. His reading glasses sat on top of them. On a mat next to the door were his brother's boots, still caked with crumbling white dirt. Pictures of him and Maggie lined the walls.

Dick walked with his drink and looked at the pictures again. He'd seen them all before, many times over, but he couldn't bother Maggie by turning on the TV and there wasn't anything else to do. There were pictures of Maggie and his brother when they were younger, one of the two of them dancing and the other of them hiking through a redwood forest.

His brother looked so much like him that Dick could hardly stand it. Sometimes it was like looking at himself. And there he was, his arm around Maggie's shoulders and drawing her closer. Planting his lips right there on her cheek. The only difference was in their chins. His brother had a nicely rounded chin that seemed to stretch his face just the smallest bit while Dick had a square jaw that filled out and cut across at a right angle.

There was one picture he always looked at more

than the rest. It was a picture of his brother shaving in the bathroom. His cheeks were covered in shaving cream and Maggie was standing to his side, her lips painted dark red. She had that chin of his in her fingers and she looked happier than anyone he'd ever seen before.

Waiting for Maggie to get off the phone with his mother, Dick stared at the picture for a good long while. He wasn't sure what it was about that picture in particular, but every week he found a way to look at it. He would excuse himself from the table or to the bathroom and stop along the way to stare at it for as long as he could. He took turns closing each eye and seeing how different it looked. There were even times he thought about sliding it into his coat and taking it home.

I know, Maggie said into the phone. He's been gone seven years and it still feels like yesterday.

Dick took the picture off the wall and carried it with him. He walked, with the picture and his drink, and went into the bathroom. He turned on the light and looked at the shower in the corner. Maggie had hung her brassieres there to dry. There was a black one, a beige one, a white one. He put the picture and his drink down on the sink and reached over and touched the white brassiere. He felt how it felt. He let go.

He looked into the medicine cabinet, Dick did. He found some pills of Maggie's and everything his brother had left behind. A stick of deodorant.   Toothbrush. Some tonic to grow hair. Then, on the middle shelf, he saw a razor and a canister of shaving cream. He picked up the razor and saw there were stray hairs between the blades. The metal top of the shaving cream canister was starting to rust.

Positioning the picture of his brother and Maggie on the sink, he pressed the button on the canister of shaving cream and filled his palm. It looked like a cloud in his hand. He leaned his head out the door and listened. Maggie had moved into the living room and was still talking to his mom, saying how she had felt, in her heart, that when she opened the door, when she got home, her husband, his brother, would be waiting there, reading one of his magazines. Dick squished the shaving cream in his hands, rubbed it into a lather.

While applying it to his face he thought of his brother, his older brother, and how he had taught him to shave. Their father had been a rotten sonuvabitch of a man and had left before they could really remember anything. Loaded up that Chevy of his and took off for greener pastures.

Gotta get you a good layer, his brother had said, smashing the shaving cream onto his face when Dick was twelve, when his brother was fourteen. Give yourself a beard of shaving cream, he said.

Dick gave himself a beard of shaving cream and looked at himself in the mirror. He couldn't tell there was any difference between him and his brother.

Get your razor, his brother had said, grabbing one of the disposable ones their dad had left behind. Pull it slowly over your beard, his brother had said.

Dick pulled the razor, his brother's razor, across his shaving cream beard. He moved it slowly until the entirety of his shaving cream beard was gone. He looked at himself in the mirror, clean-shaven, his pink skin glowing in the dull glow of the bathroom light. He looked younger without the shaving cream beard, without all that stubble. He compared himself to the picture of his brother, the one with Maggie in it, saw the difference remained in their chins, and put it back down on the sink. Before he left he rinsed the sink and the razor and touched the white brassiere again and turned out the light.

He's leaving, he heard Maggie saying into the phone. Thanks for coming by, she said. Next week? she said.

Next week, Dick lied, letting the door shut behind him.

✪ PUNCH-FOR-PUNCH ✪

THE SIMPLE TRUTH of it is one day I woke up in a house. It was a nice house. Nicer than any house I'd ever lived in before or any I ever thought I'd end up in. I woke up and there was coffee waiting and a good place to sit outside and read and drink that coffee. All of a sudden everything crummy that'd ever happened to me, all of those terrible times, they seemed like they belonged to somebody else, like they were something I'd watched on a bad TV movie.

That's how I explained it to Trudy. How I tried to explain it, anyway. Every time I started getting into it, every time I'd get her sitting down, she'd just put her hand on mine and tell me not to worry anymore.

You're safe now, she'd say.

She'd say, You made it.

She was right. Of course she was right. She was right about damn near everything. Health insurance. Loans. What color to paint the bedroom. She was right so much I started forgetting she could ever be wrong. I started thinking maybe she was the one who said let there be light and put together the sun and the stars like a casserole on Sunday.

But I still couldn't help but see signs of impending doom everywhere I looked.

In balls of cat hair in the corners.

Lines of ants on the sidewalk.

Dreams where I'd wake up and see faces looming over me in the dark.

Calm down, she'd say. There's nothing there.

But then the ceiling leaked. A big bubble grew by the stairs. Drips of water fell down onto the hardwood floors and puddles sprouted out of the cracks.

We'll call the landlord, she said. Just try and get some rest.

But I couldn't rest. Maybe I have an illness. I've always thought I had an illness. Some kind of cancer or rare new disease that's not even on the books yet. Sometimes I start thinking about what it'd be like to break a bone and I sit there thinking about it and thinking about it until I feel pressure and I'm just sure it's going to snap in two if I think about it another second more.

I was trying to tell a guy I met at the bar down the street about it. We were sitting at the bar in Mr. Mouse and he was drinking a beer with ice and salt and I just had a beer with some Lexington on the side. I told him and he rolled up his shirtsleeve and showed me a scar.

You see that there? he said. Compound fracture. Nineteen-eighty-nine. My girl shoved me off a ladder. Went to break my fall and snap.

That's just awful, I said, already imagining a bone

tearing through my skin.

You ever actually break a bone? he asked me.

No, I said. Torn some cartilage. Cracked one or two.

You ever break somebody else's?

I thought about it. Yeah, I said. Buddy of mine. We were going punch-for-punch and his nose broke like a light bulb.

I tell you what, the guy said and threw back what was left of his beer, I ain't gone punch-for-punch in a long ass time.

That's how we ended up out on the bar's porch. We cleared out a space among the tables and traded blows while the other drunks smoked and watched. His first one hit me right in the ear and I lost all sense of hearing for a while. I was thinking about my buddy and when I hit the guy it was right there in his nose. I heard it crunch and then some blood leaked out.

Pretty damn good, the guy said and took out his handkerchief to dab up some of the blood. He laid it on a nearby table where somebody had left a glass of melted ice and liquor and swallowed it down. It's not broken though, he said. Do me a favor and break the goddamn thing. Break it to the point it don't look right anymore.

I shrugged. When a man asks you to break his nose you don't have much choice in the matter. So I got to work. Grabbed his collar and just started pouring in the shots. His nose was making all kinds of sounds and bleeding to beat the band, but for some reason I just couldn't break it.

He looked at me, bloody, his eyes filled with tears. What the hell? he said. You sure you've done this before?

Yeah, I said and gave it another go. I said, I'll be damned.

We gave up a little bit after that. It didn't take long to figure out I was incapable of breaking that guy's nose. I felt like I'd let him down. I felt like I'd let myself down. I paid both of our tabs and hit the sidewalk. All the young kids and drunks walking past me seemed to know what I'd done. They spit at my feet, whispered under their breath.

I got home and worked my key into the door. Trudy was in the kitchen cooking dinner. It was going to be a nice one: roasted chicken, glazed carrots, green beans with ham. She saw me come in and dropped her apron and spoon and rushed up.

Are you okay, love? she said, touching my face.

I'm fine, I said and moved away. In the refrigerator was a case of my favorite beer she always picked up at the store. I grabbed one and tried to twist off the cap. It wasn't a twist-off though and I had to find the can opener in one of the drawers. The drawer was lined with a designer lining. Every fork and spoon and knife was in its place too. The can opener was right where it was supposed to be.

I popped open the bottle and threw the can opener at the wall. It hit with a clunk and tore a little hole in the wallpaper Trudy had bought from JC Penney. I can't stand this shit, I said.

Trudy looked hurt. What shit? she said. What can you not stand?

This, I said and gestured toward everything. The wallpaper. The apron. The dinner cooking on the stove.

The goddamn forks and the goddamn spoons and the goddamn knives and the goddamn can opener. The lining in the drawers. The beer in the fridge.

At first Trudy looked confused, but soon she sprung into action. She lit into the walls and tore the paper with her fingernails until it was hanging in threads and her nails were bleeding. Next she tossed her apron and the pots and pans into the floor. They were joined by all the utensils and liners and the mess started to grow and the juices from the food leaked out onto the floor and the juice turned dark with the dirt and tarnish and the puddle seeped out until it was nearly to the baseboards. Next she got the case of beer from the fridge and shook it until all of the bottles fell and shattered and the puddle grew with the beer and the juices and stretched from wall to wall. When she finished she stood looking at me, her chest heaving and sweat pouring off her face.

There, she said. Are you happy now?

I looked around. Looked at the floor. Looked at her.

Well, I said, no. For starters, just look at this mess.

✪ YANKEE ✪

THROUGH HAPPENSTANCE I found myself a pilgrim in The South, a sudden and bewildered owner of an old one-bedroom house in Southeastern Georgia. Across the way there was a cotton field, behind that an overgrown lot holding only a burnt-out trailer. On weekends the boys from the nearby Air Force base would pilot their Chinook helicopters over the trees, taking turns hoisting the trailer up and then dropping it back to the ground.

I used to talk to the pilots over beers at the gas station down the road. County ordinances forbade liquor and traditional bars, so the Indian who ran the Cheap-Mart set up stools and a mini-fridge in the back of his store. Between games of craps we drained mugs of skunk beer and lamented our stations in life.

Yankee, a pilot named Buck would say to me, what business do you have here? Head north. Settle in Wisconsin, Michigan. Revel in real and honest culture. Buy a snow shovel.

You've got some room to talk, I'd say. Get in your warbird over yonder and fly on out of here.

The pilots were rowdy customers. Broke bottles on the cement floor and intimidated Singh, the owner. When he finally told them to settle down they broke into an unanimous sob.

Everyday, Buck's co-pilot said. Lift. Release.

Up and down, Buck said. You lift the trailer, you drop the trailer. If only there was a war to save us from this terrible circle.

When I settled my tabs with Singh the pilots would call to me, head in hands, from their stools.

Yankee, Buck would say. Head north. Jesus, man.

From my porch I considered it. There wasn't any kind of winter in Georgia, only a breather between murderous summers. There was no breeze, but the cotton moved of its own accord. I had a neighbor, a quiet mother of three, who left Polaroids of herself taped to my front door. She was fond of saying that cotton wasn't subject to natural laws.

It grows when it's hot, she said, and it grows when it's cold. There's something about that cotton we can't understand.

She lectured me often from the confines of my pullout couch. The subject was always Southern Ways, Southern Assimilation.

You pay attention, she said, and we'll make a native of you yet.

Come Saturday we'd load up and head for Augusta, Savannah, the beach. When those Chinooks came buzzing in I felt a mean urge to escape. Listening to their rotors too long was maddening. In the car I'd turn the radio to talk news, maybe a sermon, and she'd give me hell until I returned to the sputtering country stations at the low end of the dial.

How're you gonna live, she said, if you don't immerse?

Darling, I'd say, it might surprise you to learn that life exists outside Dixie.

At the beach we'd fill coolers with beer and carry our blankets out onto the sand. We did this into November, me in my hat and bermudas and she in her bright red two-piece. I bronzed and graded papers while she turned front to back and nursed her drink.

It could always be like this, she said. You and me. The boiling, mad ocean.

I said it could, but knew it to be a lie. Her three boys were nearly of age and her husband's suspicion grew. The party had no way of lasting.

And it didn't. The Polaroids stopped one morning and I knew that was that. In their place came a long and winding note. An apology. Dearest, it read, there are forces and responsibilities which are so easily forgotten.

Before I finally retreated north, I asked the pilots if I could go up in their copter. On a Saturday morning I stood at the edge of the cotton field and watched them buzz over the trees. The machine was like a giant insect, sturdy and vicious, settling down in the dirt a few yards away. The world was wind, the air full of the yet-young cotton. With Buck's help I climbed aboard.

We raised back into the sky and I watched the earth pull away. From our highest point in the sky I could see everything. My roof. Angie's roof. The Cheap-Mart, the town square, the college. There was everything and nothing. A land too familiar and too foreign to name.

Buck's mechanical voice buzzed over the intercom. You want at the hoist? he said.

I crawled along the metal belly into the cockpit and grabbed the jack controls. On the radar screen was that burnt-out trailer. A glowing green rectangle, full and complete, no rust or holes or anything.

You'll feel the weight, Buck's voice buzzed. You'll feel it as soon as the hook holds and you pull back.

He was right and he was wrong. The Chinook dipped and sank as we hauled that load––that much was true––but as that trailer wrenched near, and as I saw it float off the ground and away from the weeds and renegade grass, there was simply no weight at all.

✪ OUTLAWS ✪

FAYE AND ME were really up a creek. The rent was due and collection companies were ringing the phone every couple of minutes. My problems all stemmed from my second divorce and the child support I couldn't afford in the first place. Credit cards were the source of Faye's. She liked to shop a little too much and it'd caught up with her. So we did what we had to do. We pooled what money there was and Faye maxed out her last pair of cards. We loaded her wardrobe into the car and took off with no real direction.

For two days we just drove around pretending to be outlaws. I handled the wheel and Faye the map. She got into the habit, between painting and repainting her toenails, of reading off names of all these small towns we could settle down in.

Harpersburg, she said. Maybe Murfreesboro. You know how I love Tennessee.

I didn't know she loved Tennessee. We'd only been together a few months and I didn't know much about her at all, but she was always assuming I knew this thing or that. She was a helluva good-looking woman though, so I played along most times.

Tennessee's just about your favorite, I said.

Hell yes, she said, shifting up on her knees in the passenger seat. Lakes and mountains. Countryside. She squealed and stretched, her white tank top lifting up and over her flat stomach, revealing the once-hot pink, now faded to fuchsia, butterfly tattoo on her hip.

Hey Butterfly, I said to her.

Hey Sugar-pie, she said back.

You wanna settle down in Tennessee?

You mean it? she said, clapping. You'd live there?

Wherever you want, I said. I reached over and put my hand on the fat of her thigh.

That's what I want, she said.

Afterwards we stopped at a liquor store down the road and bought the cheapest six-packs they had. We were in a small town on the back roads of Indiana, and when I asked the kid working the register how to get to Tennessee he just shrugged and said, Drive south.

Back in the car we popped open a couple beers and toasted our new lives. Faye said she wanted to maybe start singing when we got established.

You know how I always wanted to be a country singer, she said. Like Loretta Lynn.

Sure, I said, though I hadn't known that either.

People always said I had a voice just about as good as hers, she said, and then she got to singing Loretta's songs.

I settled in with my beer, keeping eye for police, and listened as she got to belting out Don't Come Home

A'Drinkin'. Faye didn't have the best voice I'd ever heard, that was for sure. It was pitchy and she liked to warble on, but I could tell she was putting every last bit of herself into that song and I couldn't help but smile.

That sure was pretty, I said when she was done.

Really? she said. You really think so?

Just about the best I ever heard.

Oh honey, she said, leaning over and wrapping her arms around my neck. She gave my cheek a big, wet kiss and then asked me, What do you wanna do down in Tennessee?

I don't know, I said, pausing for a slug. Might be a coal miner.

Uh huh, she said. Sure.

I mean it, I said with a wink. You or Loretta know anything about that kind of life?

Faye giggled and started in on Coal Miner's Daughter. I was happy that she got to singing because the last thing I wanted to do was talk about the future. Things had been so awful, what with my ex-wife being a monster and all of Faye's bills, that I didn't know for shit what I wanted after the smoke cleared. Didn't even know if I wanted to keep on with Faye, to be honest.

See, Faye was an absolute saint of a woman. Kind, funny, understanding to a fault, but she was young, eight years my junior, and she lacked a certain seriousness about her. Everything to her was solvable, temporary, and the gravity of our situation––how much we'd fucked things up, how much we owed, and what a general shit-storm we were in––didn't seem to bother her for a second. Being with her then was like looking down one day and realizing you were sporting a fancy convertible when what you really needed was a four-door sedan.

That's what I was thinking when we pulled into a motel off the road. It was a small, six-room place with a dried-up pool and a rusted sign that just said MOTEL. The doors were all aqua blue and so was the trimming. There wasn't another car parked in the lot. I got out and walked over to the office where, at the desk, was this sad looking guy with a half-grown-in beard. Across one of his cheeks was this big, purple birthmark.

Hot one out there, I said, filling out a form.

You ain't kiddin', he said. Been burnin' up all week.

Ain't that the truth. Say, I said, pretty slow around here?

Always is, he said, reaching under the counter and pulling out a beer. Don't get much business.

I said, You own this place?

Sure do, he said. Well, it was my mom's and when she passed I took over.

How long's that been? I said.

Six years now, he said. Bout that.

Huh, I said.

It ain't too bad, he said. Hardly anybody comes through and I just stay over here in Six. He sipped his beer then and shook his head. Don't worry though. I got you two in One, so I won't be in your hair at all.

Well, I said, thank ya. We'll be out of your way tomorrow, or the day after at the latest.

Stay long as you like, he said. He had that beer to his lips but he wasn't drinking. I could see him staring out the window with his eyes fixed on Faye, who was fanning herself by the car. Ain't no hurry.

Faye and me got in our room and took turns in the shower. When I got out, and was toweling off, she was sitting there on the bed wearing this light blue bikini covered in black butterflies.

How about that? I said.

I got it before we took off, she said. It was on-sale at the K-Mart and I figured it wouldn't hurt anything if I wasn't gonna pay my bills anymore.

Not gonna hurt anything, I said.

Well good, she said. Glad you think so.

The two of us tussled on the bed and then in the floor until the sun went down and night rolled in. When we were done Faye went straight to sleep, that blue bikini hanging from her like ropes, and that left me to sit there thinking over everything. I'd been tied down by work and Nat, my ex, for so long I didn't quite know how to handle all the freedom I had all of a sudden. So I sat there dreaming of places I could go, things I could do, until I'd had my fill and closed my eyes.

IN THE MORNING Faye was gone. My first thought was that she'd skipped town. First I was shocked by the relief I felt. But soon after, I got to worrying that something had happened.

I threw on some clothes and opened the door, only to find the fella with the purple birthmark sitting in a lawn chair outside. He was drinking a beer and had a whole case's worth chilling in a cooler at his feet.

Mornin', he said. You lookin' for Faye?

Yeah, I said, feeling uneasy hearing her name in his mouth. Where'd she wander off to?

Yonder, he said and pointed to a patch of trees across the road. She's picking strawberries.

Strawberries?

Yeah, he said, have you a seat. He pointed at an empty lawn chair and handed me a beer after I'd sat down. We got to talkin' this mornin' and I told her there was a mess of wild strawberries over there.

Okay, I said, popping open my beer. They safe to eat?

Hell yes, he said. They're just strawberries.

We sat there drinking beer and watching a car go by every twenty minutes or so. It felt so lonesome I could barely stand it. Not trying to shit on your parade, I said, but do you ever get tired of living out in the middle of nowhere?

The owner nodded slowly, like it was a question he wondered himself. It's slow as a motherfucker, he said. Bout put you to sleep half the time.

No doubt, I said. I looked across the road, at that patch of trees, and thought I could see a glimpse of Faye out there. Hey Butterfly, I yelled.

Hey Sugar-pie, she called back through the trees.

It's got its good parts though, the owner said.

Yeah? I said. What's that?

Bein' out here, he said, it's freeing, I guess. All I got to do is sit on my ass and drink beer and wait.

There're worse jobs, I said.

I'll drink to that, he said and took a healthy swig. When he was done he got another beer out of the cooler and popped it open. I mean, I get a ton of time to think and dick around. Most people can't say that.

No they can't, I said.

And, he said, I don't get many people here, but I get a few. Sometimes I get a newlywed couple out here and they lodge up a while.

I looked at him and watched him drink his beer. Between the piss-poor beard he was sporting and that birthmark on his cheek I figured this here was a lonely man. So lonely that the thought of a couple kids, fresh off being hitched, coming in and screwing all over the place probably made him sad as hell.

I got a story for you, he said out of nowhere. Hey, for starters, what's your name, buddy?

White, I said.

Well, White, he said, my name's Barry. And this was probably a year ago. Last summer, anyway. This group of bikers rolled in one weekend. Must've been a dozen of 'em, all riding on these big, shiny bikes.

These weekend warriors or real, honest bikers? I said.

Oh, Barry said, these were outlaws. The real deal. And I told 'em I didn't have enough rooms for all of 'em, and they just said one would be fine.

All twelve in one room? I said.

That's right, Barry said. They were sleeping on the floor, in the closet, in the bathtub. Everywhere. But that's not my point.

What's the point? I said.

Well, Barry said, they had this girl with 'em. Just one. She was maybe the prettiest girl I'd ever seen. Dark hair. Grey eyes. Walked around here in this long, white number, like a wedding dress.

She was a looker, huh? I said.

Oh god, he said. White, this woman was magical. Barry lifted his beer and drank long and hard. I couldn't hardly talk to her for how beautiful she was.

What happened to her? I said.

I don't know, Barry said. I try not to think about what happened in that room.

Sounds like a good idea, I said, trying to keep from doing it myself.

But that's not the point, he said. Point is that it's lonely, but every now and then someone comes along and makes it all worth it.

Right then Faye climbed out of the patch of trees. She had on her bikini top and cut-offs and was carrying a Wal-Mart bag full of strawberries.

You find a whole bunch? I said.

We're gonna eat so good tonight, she said as she crossed the road. I thought maybe I'd cut these up and we could get some steaks in town. Thought we could really do it up.

That sounds about perfect, I said.

You're more'n welcome to join us, she said to Barry.

Nah, Barry said. I got a microwave dinner with my name on it.

Come on, Faye said and sat the sack down by the cooler. We insist, don't we?

She looked at me and then Barry looked at me too. I shrugged. Yeah, I said. We insist.

Well shit, Barry said, smiling like he couldn't of been more pleased. That's mighty kind of you.

The rest of the day I sat in that lawn chair next to Barry and me and him and Faye shot the shit and drank beer. She was telling him everything she could think of. About her favorite places to shop and where she grew up and how she never really felt good before I came along.

I was seeing this piece of shit named Todd, she told him. And Todd was mean as a striped-snake. Use to get liquored up and throw me around. Threatened to kill me on more than a few occasions.

That is a shame, Barry said, really focused on everything Faye was saying, almost like he couldn't look away. I tell you, he said, some people don't know what they have.

No they don't, Faye said. And you know I can't stand that.

I do, Barry said.

And White here, she said, he knew Todd from a ways back. Use to play cards, didn't you hon?

We did, I said.

That's right, she said. And he was over there one night playing cards and he caught Todd pulling me round by the hair. Didn't you? I nodded. She said, Tell him what you did.

I laid him out, I said.

You sure as shit did, she said.

Thatta boy, Barry said, taking his eyes off Faye.

And what'd you say to me? he said.

I said, Let's get out of here.

She said, That's right. Let's get out of here. And we did. She leaned down and gave me a kiss on the lips. We been together ever since.

That's the long and short of it, I said.

Which was true, but not true at all. I didn't want to

get into the specifics of things. I didn't want to spoil the party by finally coming clean and letting Faye know that Todd, one of the worst gamblers in the history of cards, had bet her on a flush that didn't make. And I didn't want to tell her I laid him out after he welched on that bet and lost his damn mind. Didn't seem like something I really needed to get into, particularly after I'd really taken a shine to her.

But it wasn't like I'd planned the whole thing turning out the way it did. When Todd put her on the line, to cover a thirty-dollar bet, I thought maybe I'd get a night's worth out of her and bring her back the next day. When we got in my car though, after I'd put him on his ass, she reached across the console and stroked my hand. Then she held it and started smiling like she'd never been happier before.

They fit, she said to me and looked at our knotted fingers. I've been looking a long time for something that fits.

I was running that over in my head while she talked to Barry, telling him every little story from every little day we'd spent together, and I really think Barry would've sat there listening to Faye for as long as she would've talked, but the morning started its crawl into afternoon and we all got hungry. Finally we decided to go with Faye's plan and eat those strawberries and grill up some steak. Faye borrowed my knife and got to work on those strawberries while Barry and me got in my car and drove to the IGA in town to get steaks and some more beer.

I didn't have hardly a dime to my name so Barry bought a half-dozen T-bones from the butcher and I sprung for half of another case of beer. It had the makings of a fine night, all things considered, but as we were walking across the parking lot Barry nudged me with his elbow and said, Hey, that pretty girl of yours have a sister?

What's that? I said. I was opening my trunk and putting the beer in.

Faye, he said. She's just about the prettiest girl ever.

Prettier than that girl with the bikers? I said, getting behind the wheel.

Oh, he said, it's not even a contest. Not meaning to step on your toes, White, just lettin' you know you got somethin' magical ridin' round with you.

I appreciate that, I said. Really do.

I didn't though. There ain't no way to appreciate some complete stranger making comments like that. I mean, I'd seen the way he'd been watching her, how he hung on her every word, and right then my defenses kicked in and I was ready to leave by the time we pulled back in at the motel.

Faye had a spread set up though. She'd pulled a table out of our room and covered it with a towel and had paper plates and plastic forks and spoons put out. The ice bucket held the strawberries.

Look at this, Barry said, loading the cooler with the beer we'd bought.

Yeah, I said. Look at this.

Figure we could use a celebration, Faye said. New lives, new friends.

New lives, Barry repeated. New friends.

Barry found a small charcoal grill in a shed behind the motel and we got some coals firing and before too long we were drinking beers and cooking those steaks. Those two seemed to be having a hell of a good time. Faye kept telling her stories and Barry kept listening and I kept my distance for the most part. What he'd said to me had put me on edge and I didn't want to get too chummy in case I had to whip his ass and make a run for it.

How's that cow? he said from the table. Him and Faye were between stories while I cooked.

Just about done, I said, grabbing a plate and popping down one of those steaks.

The three of us sat down and tried damn hard to cut the meat with those plastic knives and forks. It got to be a pretty big joke, how useless they were, and Faye kept saying it was just about the most appropriate thing ever, three full-time losers sitting down to such a fine meal and not having anything to get the job done.

Here, I said, getting my knife out again. Pass her around.

That steak, once we got it carved down to size, was delicious. The strawberries were good too, sweet and juicy, and we all had more than our fill and had to sit back with our bellies hanging out. We were smiling and not talking much because we were too full to do much of anything. I looked over at Faye and she looked like the prettiest girl who ever came around, just like Barry had said. I appreciated her then, what I'd had, and I wanted to let her know.

Hey, I said, nudging her with my foot. Tell Barry here what you're wanting to do when you get down to Tennessee.

Oh, she said, he doesn't want to hear that.

Sure I do, Barry said and promptly sat straight up.

Really? she said.

Really, he said. Really really.

Just tell him, I said. He really wants to know.

Well, she said, if I'm going to be honest, I want to be a singer.

Like Loretta Lynn? he said.

Faye's face lit up like a light bulb. Just like Loretta Lynn, she said.

Loretta was my mom's favorite, Barry said. Hold on a sec. I've got an idea.

He rushed off and disappeared into his office. By then the sun was low in the sky and shadows were crawling across the parking lot. Faye drunkenly got out of her lawn chair and came over to me and leaned down. She gave me a weak kiss and struggled to keep her eyes open. You having a good time? she asked.

Sure, I said.

Barry's a heckuva guy, right? she said.

Heckuva guy, I said.

What's wrong? she said.

Nothing, I said. I took her hand like she had taken mine that night I won her from Todd. Nothing at all.

I mean it, she said, looking scared. What's wrong?

Nothing, I said. I mean it, nothing is wrong.

Is this strange? she said. This whole thing?

I thought about that question. I could've said yes, I could've blown the lid off the whole situation, but I looked at her––sweet, sweet Faye, my Butterfly––and shook my head. Not strange at all, I said.

Okay, she said. If you want to leave tomorrow, I'm fine with that.

38

Maybe, I said. We'll see.

Barry hurried back to us with an armful of records. He put them on the table and we could see in the dim light that there were all kinds of Loretta Lynn albums. Seemed like he had every one she'd ever put out.

I told you, he said. Mom loved her Loretta. We used to sit in that office and listen all day.

You got a record player in there? Faye said.

We did, Barry said. Haven't played it in ages though. Haven't had a reason. Don't know if it even works anymore.

Faye looked in the direction of the office and got this look like she was thinking something over. You got any extension cords?

Tons, Barry said.

Go get 'em, she said. I got an idea.

Barry took off again, this time toward the shed, and Faye went to the office and came out carrying that record player Barry'd been talking about. It was a big unit, but small enough that Faye could bring it with her back to the table. I cleared off the plates and the ice bucket.

Figured we could use some tunes, she said.

Just what we needed, I said.

Hey, she said to me before leaning in and giving me another kiss. How you doing, Sugar-pie?

Doing great, Butterfly, I said.

Good, she said.

A few minutes later Barry came back with a cluster of extension cords. He handed them to Faye, who snaked them back to our room and plugged them into the outlet that powered our TV. That record player popped on, the face of it coming alive and flashing the time. It blinked all zeroes until Barry punched a couple buttons and then opened the top. He got to spinning one of those records and Loretta Lynn burst through the speakers.

Hot damn, Barry said, thrilled.

That's just what we needed, Faye said and gave me a wink.

That's right, I said.

Her and Barry sat in the lawn chairs and drank more beer and sang every word of every song. When it came time to flip the record Barry flipped it and they sang every song on that side. When that record ran out, Barry got another from the pile and they sang every word on that one, too. Then Barry stopped. He wasn't singing anymore. This was on the third record maybe. He was too busy listening to Faye at that point.

This one's got talent, he said to me. Am I right?

You are right, I said. I was on my last beer. Real talent, I said.

She's gonna make it, by god, Barry said.

She is, I said.

They finished that record and, like clockwork, Barry got the next album off the pile and put it on. The needle dropped and Faye didn't miss a beat. Her and Loretta were singing together, to be sure, and they were making beautiful music. I lasted as long as I could. I finished my beer and felt a full-day's worth slogging around in my head. I was tired from all the driving, all the sun, all the booze, and I told the two of them that I needed to take a quick siesta. Barry told me to stick around, and Faye said she didn't want me to leave, but I just shook his hand and gave her a quick peck on the cheek.

You keep having yourselves a time, I said, walking toward our room. Don't mind me a bit.

I got into bed and pulled the sheets over my head, but that didn't block them out. I could still hear Faye and Loretta singing and Barry clapping and going on about how good she sounded. Somewhere in the middle of the night, maybe five more albums into the stack, I finally drifted off and got some rest.

That next morning I got up and threw my clothes back on. I planned on leaving one way or another so I packed up my bag and combed my hair in the mirror. I brushed my teeth and patted myself down with some soap and water. Outside Faye and Barry were passed out in those lawn chairs. The record player, still being plugged in, hummed in the still summer air. From the doorway I could see that Faye's hand, the one that had crossed my console, the one that had fit mine, was locked with Barry's. He was smiling in his sleep and so was she, his birthmark and her butterfly glowing just a little in the morning sun.

I didn't bother waking them. I got in my car and put it in neutral so it could roll out into the road. There was no reason to start the engine or make any noise. When you play cards long enough you learn the deal. You got to be honest with yourself and put away your pride. Recognize when the fella sitting across from you is holding the better hand.

You got to learn how to fold.

✪ SOME KIND OF PLAN ✪

WHEN JACKSON WOKE in the middle of the night all he knew of the world was thirst. He made his way through the darkened house and into the kitchen. The dream he'd been having was something about driving a truck through a desert. It'd been a vivid one, a dream full of panic.

In the kitchen he opened the cabinet that held their glasses and pulled out one of the tall blue ones they'd bought in a set from JC Penney years before. Next he was in the freezer and grappling for the ice try, which, when he found it, was empty save for four solitary cubes. He cursed Lena, his wife, for never filling it, and cracked it over the counter.

In the dark he heard the cubes smack against the counter and heard one of them slip onto the floor. Damn it, he said, and kicked at it. When he filled his glass with the cubes and some water from the tap, he carried it into the living room and sat on the couch.

The early thud of a hangover beat against his

temples. Clay had been over earlier, walked across the street with a bottle of Jim Beam and said he needed to talk. Jackson, he said, settling in a chair by the couch, I'm just at the end of my rope. Every time Vicki and me get to talking about the future or what's wrong, she just clams up and won't say a word. It's like it's the last thing she wants to get into.

He sat there in the dark, Jackson did, and looked at where he'd placed his glass of water. The house was pitch-black and all he could see were shadows thrown by the street light from outside. It was quiet too, the only sound the ice settling and whining in the water.

Love is about communication, he'd said to Clay. He had a glass full of whiskey then and was taking long, slow drags. That's one thing me and Lena have learned. You've got to talk, Clay. If you don't you're in trouble.

Thinking about the conversation, about drinking the whiskey, gave him a shiver so vile he had to stand up from the couch. He grabbed his glass of water and downed it, but was still thirsty. He went back to the tap and listened to it fill again.

Back in the living room, he stopped by the picture window near the front door and peeled back the curtain. The world was just as quiet outside as it was in. All the houses, for as far as he could see, had no lights. Clay and Vicki's house was black too. You're the only person awake anywhere, he thought as he took a gulp of water.

I'm really in a bad way here, Clay had said. He hadn't drank so much as he'd watched Jackson drink. Instead he'd turned his glass around in his hands. My old man told me once, he said, there comes a time when you've got to take stock and count your losses.

That's good advice, Jackson had said. Maybe it's time you two have a good, long talk. Figure out where you're both at and make some kind of plan.

A plan, Clay said back to him. Yes sir, that's probably a good idea.

Jackson was running that through his mind, the way Clay had said it, when the phone by the couch rang a single time. That was the signal, had been for the last three months.

He dialed the numbers, a reflex at that point, and waited. It didn't ring on his end of the line before he heard the other pick up.

Hello, Vicki whispered.

Hi Love, he said, whispering himself.

I can't talk, she said, but I thought I should call.

Okay, he said. He through the window and saw that Clay and Vicki's house was still black. How're things over there?

I don't know, she said in a tone he couldn't read. Lots of talking. I'm tired, worn out honestly, but I woke up and thought I should call.

It's all right, he whispered, though he wasn't sure if it was.

She said, Well, I don't have much to say, and he heard her light a cigarette and inhale. I should get off here.

You do what you need to do, Jackson said. Can we meet in a couple of days? Maybe get something to eat?

I don't think so, she answered and inhaled a second time. I think we're going to see Clay's parents this weekend. It's some kind of plan of his. I don't know.

44

A plan, Jackson said.

Anyway, Vicki said, I just wanted to call, Jackson. I just thought it was fair. I'll talk to you soon, she said.

When? he said, reaching for his glass of water.

I don't know, she said. Soon.

She was gone then and he hung up the phone. Across the street a light blinked on and then shut off just as quickly. Jackson sat and waited for it to go on again, but gave up a few minutes later.

After that he sat on the couch in the dark and drank his water. It was cold and felt good in his throat. The hangover was still thudding around though, and he knew he should get more water after he'd finished his glass, but he couldn't make himself stand. He was thinking about the dream he'd been having, something about driving a truck through the desert. He wondered where he'd been going and felt like at some point in the dream he had known.

IT COMES
✪ WITH THE TERRITORY ✪

LISTEN HERE, Les said into the phone, if I ever find out who this is I'm going to kick your head in.

Who is it? Eve said, walking into the front room.

You know who the hell it is, Les said.

Is that her? the voice on the phone said. Is that that fine piece of ass?

Kick your head in, Les said again and threw the phone at the wall. It exploded into a shower of plastic and circuitry.

That's the fourth one this month, Eve said. Honey––

Don't honey me, Les said and went to get his coat from the closet. I'm sick of it. Sick to goddamn death.

It's not my fault, Eve said and weakly crossed her arms. I promise honey, I didn't do anything.

The hell you didn't, he said. He had his coat on and was reaching for his keys. If you didn't, who did?

I don't know, she said. Somebody in town? An ex-boyfriend? A drunk?

It's always somebody else, Les said. The buck's always passed on, right?

No, she said and moved to cross the room, her arms already reaching for him. Stay in, she said. Don't leave.

The other phone, this one in the kitchen, rang then.

Honey, she said.

Well, he said, opening the door, you'd better damn well go and answer it.

Les slammed the door behind him and got in his truck. As he pulled out he saw Eve standing at the window, her face already wet with tears. He made his way into town, past the Ponderosa and the Kroger's, and parked in a strip-mall lot that housed El Capitan, the Mexican restaurant, Jo-Anne's Fabrics, and a party store that'd been closed for two years. At the end of the building was Johnnie's, the only bar in town.

Given it was a Tuesday night, Johnnie's was empty save for the bartender, a fella named Gillan who Les knew from high school. Les got him a seat at the bar and ordered two Miller Lite's. He drank the first one in three gulps and sipped the second.

How's business? Gillan asked.

Same bullshit, Les said.

Different day, Gillan said.

Ain't that the truth, Les said. Say, any chance you could put on the Bucks' game?

Sure thing, Gillan said. He put down a lime he'd been slicing and grabbed a remote from under the bar. His thumb flipped through the channels until he landed on the game. The Bucks were playing the Knicks in New

York and were already down by ten. I don't know why you torture yourself, Gillan said, shaking his head.

You and me both, Les said. He finished his second beer, watched a Knick player swish a three from five feet behind the line, and ordered another couple of Miller Lite's.

Gillan got the pair of beers from a cooler and popped their tops. He set them in front of Les and took the empties. In a hurry tonight, he said.

You got it, Les said. On the TV Milwaukee's center dribbled straight into a double-team. Way things're going, Les said, I can't hardly leave the house.

How you figure? Gillian said.

Shit, Les said, some bunch of fellas been calling and asking for Eve. Bunch of goddamn perverts.

No kidding, Gillian said.

I can't sleep for it. They come all hours. Two, three in the morning. Doesn't matter. Saying shit you wouldn't believe.

No shit, Gillian said.

Some of 'em, Les said, they just breathe. You can hear what they're doing. Clear as day.

That right there, Gillian said, that's a bad situation. I mean, someone started calling Janice like that? I'd probably kill 'em.

You're telling me, Les said.

Think she's running around? Gillian was leaning toward Les with his elbows on the bar. He was whispering. I mean, is that the deal here?

No, Les said. I don't think so. Way I figure, there's somebody writing about her on a bunch of bathroom walls. Found one at the Kroger's.

What? Gillan said.

Yeah, Les said. Written right there in marker. Eve's got the best ass in town, give her a call.

Son of a bitch, Gillan said.

You said it, Les said.

Now, Gillan said, I'm gonna say something and I don't want you to take it the wrong way.

Les took another gulp of his beer. All right, he said.

I mean, that's the last thing I want.

No, Les said. No, I won't.

All right, Gillan said. I just want to put it out there. I mean, you went and married the best looking girl in town. Everybody knows that.

Okay, Les said.

Back in school she was all there was, Gillan said. I remember she was all anyone wanted to talk about.

What're you getting at? Les said. He gripped the neck of his beer.

Nothing, Gillan said. Just that something like this? Maybe it comes with the territory.

Les looked at Gillan, who already seemed to regret what he'd said. Then he looked at the TV and saw a huddle of exhausted Bucks in a timeout. I'm going to the pisser, Les said and released his grip on the bottle. I'm gonna come back, settle up, and pretend this conversation never happened.

Yeah, Gillan said embarrassed. Maybe that's best.

Yep, Les said and got up.

Les, Gillan said, I'm sorry, buddy. I didn't mean nothing.

Nope, Les said, you didn't mean a thing.

In the bathroom Les picked the stall near the back

and locked the door. He unzipped his jeans and braced himself against the wall while he pissed for a long time.

It comes with the territory, he said to himself, mid-stream.

When he finished he zipped up and flushed and thought of Gillan in high school, acne-ridden and chubby in the gut with hips like a teapot. And then he thought of Eve, a knockout who walked the halls on his arm and kept an army of pissants and losers like Gillan shooting in their pants.

With the stall still locked, Les took a marker from his back pocket and quickly wrote on the door EVE'S GOT THE FINEST PUSS IN TOWN and jotted their number underneath.

When he got back to the bar an apologetic Gillan told him he was gonna buy his beers. I swear, he said, I really didn't mean anything a few minutes ago. Just got to talking, you know?

Yeah, Les said and made for the door, I know how it is. Before he left he turned back. I know just how it is, he said again, making sure to check the score on the TV one last time.

✪ COMING HOME ✪

AFTER WEEKS of negotiating, my wife Vanessa finally agreed to let me come home. I'd been holed up in a Best Western on the other side of town, getting my dinners from the drive-thru's and washing clothes in the sink. Half the time I spent camped out on the bed, drinking until I couldn't drink anymore. The other half was with my girlfriend Mackenzie, whom my wife wound up discovering via a moment of absentmindedness on my part. That could be forgiven, my wife said. Everything could be washed over and forgotten about, I could come home and be with my family once again, if only I said goodbye to Mackenzie and that time in my life.

All things considered, it seemed like a rather sweet deal, but something about giving up that girl didn't sit too well with me. Vanessa said it was a typical have-your-cake-and-eat-it-too situation.

You can't have me and Bradley if you want to be with that girl, she said over the phone one night. Bradley was my four-year-old son. It comes down to this, my wife said. Either go run around with that slut and sow whatever oats you've still got, or come home and be a husband and a father. You can't have both.

But I wanted both.

There was something wonderful about sitting down for roast and vegetables with the family, drinking a glass or two of wine, helping with the dishes, and then making up some excuse as to why I had to go back to the office—papers to grade, classes to prep—and then choking the life out of the evening by crawling bars with Mackenzie and her hot-tempered friends. It was the best of both worlds, the perfect combination of ice and fire that made my life so very enjoyable. When I was at home, listening to Vanessa go on about whatever Bradley had done that afternoon, or Bradley talking about the backyard and the animals and insects who lived there, I was perfectly content, but I still longed to be out and about, my arm wrapped around my pretty young girl, the music pumping from the speakers while we found a dark corner and grinded against one another. When I was there, her thin, jeaned legs pumping against mine, I found myself excited about the culmination of it all—the ride home where I would dart about in an effort to avoid the authorities, my sneak into the house and into bed with Vanessa, who I knew would be ready for some messing around if only I sucked, ever so gently, on her earlobe.

I don't think you understand, I told Vanessa. You have to know I love you, love you both. This isn't a matter of that.

Well, she said, what's it a matter of, then?

Of freedom, I said. Of choice. Of taking life and

52

sculpting from it that which you want.

That didn't sit too well with her, though. Vanessa wasn't one who appreciated abstracts, things of questionable weight and application. She scoffed at the idea and said that maybe it was her fault, maybe she should've known better than to get involved with a man of letters.

It's so hard to get you to take anything seriously, she said. It's like making Bradley choose his lunch.

My son was the reason I finally relented. I was lying there at the Best Western in mid-August, picking through a tray of supermarket sushi, when I realized that the boy needed his father around. He was a sensitive soul, took after me of course, and without intervention his mother could have done irreparable damage to his susceptible psyche. I mean, here was a little boy who chose long walks over television, who cried at the sight of a particularly beautiful bird. His emotions and sensitivities were a gift to me, but sometimes they wore on Vanessa to the point of contempt.

He needs to stop sucking his thumb, she was fond of saying. See, Bradley was a thumb sucker. If left unchecked he would've sucked on his thumb from here to eternity. But Vanessa was worried about the medical problems, the looks from other parents, the inevitable notes from his teachers he would come home with after he started school. Just imagine what people are going to think, she would say.

She even found a term for it. Stereotypic Movement Disorder. She looked it up on the computer and found pictures of mangled jaws. She would stand over Bradley as he put his thumb into his mouth, or when she came across him, and say the words slowly, as if chanting. Stereo-typic-move-ment-dis-or-der. Bradley, ever the angel, would look up at her with this happy expression, his tiny thumb disappeared by his lips. We need to get this checked out, Vanessa said. We should see a doctor and get this taken care of.

How could I have left poor Bradley alone with that? How could I have abandoned him and spent the rest of my days ordering watered-down drinks at dives and pubs, trying desperately to make small talk with Mackenzie's bohemian friends just so I could continue getting into her hip-huggers? I couldn't, that's how. There was a decision to be made, a real, adult decision I had to come across if I wanted to help raise my son in an environment that somewhat resembled sanity.

So I came home. I packed up my wrinkled clothes and books and drove the five miles to the suburbs and pulled into my driveway for the first time in two months. It looked the same. Nothing was different—no new paint scheme, changed locks, nothing. I carried my bags up to the front door, knocked, and Vanessa answered. Bradley was at her hip. He smiled while she did not. They moved to the side, I walked in, put my bags by the couch, and then the three of us sat and watched a television show about a judge who solved mysteries in his spare time.

After dinner that night, as we were scrubbing dishes in the sink, Vanessa asked me if I'd broken things off with Mackenzie. Have you done it yet? was how she put it.

Tomorrow, I said. I'll drive into town and do it

tomorrow.

I don't like the idea of you going to see her, Vanessa said. I shouldn't have let you come home.

Don't worry, I said, wrapping one of my soapy arms around her waist. It won't take long. And then this whole sordid episode will be behind us.

Vanessa looked at me through squinted eyes. I could tell she didn't trust me, didn't believe what I was saying. There was a distance there I'd grown used to since she'd found a letter Mackenzie had written in one of my coat pockets. It hadn't necessarily been romantic or loving, but there was enough on the page to let her know that I'd been, for lack of a better term, running around. We'll see what happens, Vanessa said. We'll see if you do the right thing or not.

After putting away the dishes I went and took my first satisfactory shower in weeks. The unit at the Best Western had rarely kept hot water for more than a few minutes. I scrubbed and soaked and grabbed a fresh towel as I stepped out. In the mirror I looked at the scruff I'd grown out of negligence. From the cabinet I took a can of shaving cream and lathered myself. A set of new razors, unopened from the supermarket, sat in the cabinet as well. I removed one and ran it under the hot water. When I was finished I recognized myself again and ran my hands over my smooth cheeks.

Vanessa was lying on our bed when I exited the bath. Instead of her usual slip, a rose-colored number that hung tightly over her thighs, she wore a pair of pajama bottoms and a t-shirt. I had no hope of starting anything, whether I sucked on an earlobe or not, but I cuddled up to her all the same and tried to work my magic.

You're not going to get anywhere, she told me.

It's worth the try, I said.

It's not, she said. Besides, I need a favor from you.

Oh? I said, dropping my towel on the floor.

Don't get too excited, she said, reaching for a magazine on the nightstand. I really need you to talk to Bradley. Tonight. Get him to stop it with the thumb.

I bent down and picked up my towel. Why? I said. What's the harm? Let the boy suck his thumb.

He's four, she said. And it's time that he stops and gets over the whole thing.

Maybe he enjoys it, I said.

Enjoys it? Vanessa said. She set the magazine down on her chest and breathed in so deep that it raised into the air. I don't care if he enjoys it, it needs to stop. Go and talk to him. You're his father. Do something.

If I hadn't just returned from exile I would've put up more of a fight. For months we'd been having that argument and I'd always stood firm. Whenever she got after him for the sucking I'd say something like, how about we just calm down, or who really cares? It'd led to conflict after conflict, probably more so than any other subject besides Mackenzie, and I knew that if I caused a fuss that night I could've gone ahead and booked my room again at the Best Western. So, instead of standing my ground, I threw on some clothes and made my way to Bradley's room.

He was lying there on his bed when I walked in. There was a light next to him that had a rotating shade with animals cut out of the sides. It threw shapes on the walls, a zoo of giraffes and bears and rhinoceroses and everything else you could imagine, and he was lying there in the half-dark, his thumb plopped in his mouth.

There's my boy, I said to him from the doorway.

Daddy, he said, removing his thumb long enough to speak.

How's the weather in here? I said. Too cold? Too hot?

He laughed and mimicked something I'd read to him in a story before. It's juuuust right, he said.

Just right, I said. Good, good. You know, it's good to be home again, sport.

Okay, he said and smiled. He plopped his thumb back into his mouth.

Where'd you go? he said.

Away, I said. Just away for a little bit.

He rolled over onto his side and touched the shade of the lamp. But you came back, he said.

I came back, I said. Listen, your mom wants me to talk to you about something. About you sucking on your thumb. She's said something about it to you before, right?

Right, he said.

About how it's not a good thing to do?

Right.

About how big four-year-old boys shouldn't suck on their thumbs?

Right.

Okay then, I said. Then you know?

Right, he said again.

Well, I said. That means you're going to have to stop.

Okay, Daddy, he said.

I walked over to his bed and patted the lump that was his leg. He smiled big and bright despite the digit stuck between his lips. I sat down and touched his hair. I remember when your Grandma made me stop sucking my thumb, I said.

She sat me down one day and said I couldn't do it anymore. Said I was too big.

Were you sad? he asked.

Maybe, I said. That's too long to remember. But she was right. I was too old to suck on my thumb. Little kids suck on their thumbs. Little kids who don't know any better.

But I'm a little kid, Bradley said.

You are, I said. But you're not that little anymore. You'll be going to school next year, won't you? Are you still going to be sucking on your thumb when you go to school?

Bradley thought about it a second. He rolled his head back on his pillow like he was really searching for an answer. The sucking action on his thumb stopped as he gave his sole attention to the question at hand. Finally, he nodded. Yes, he said. I'm going to suck my thumb forever and forever.

I said, Well, how can I argue with that? If you're going to suck on that thumb forever and forever.

Forever and forever, he said.

I brushed the hair from his eyes and looked at him bathed in the light from his lamp. It was a great thing to see my boy after all that time, to finally sit there and take stock of my son. He was a beautiful creature, soft and vulnerable, fragile in a very real sense. I wanted to pick him up and hold him like an infant for the rest of our lives, hold him like that until I just collapsed one day from the weight of his growing frame. Tell you what, I said. You keep sucking that thumb, tonight and tomorrow. After that, though, we're going to have to put an end to it. I don't think Mommy would be too happy if we didn't.

Nope, Bradley said. I don't reckon Mommy would be too happy.

I fixed his covers and flipped off the lamp. I left him in his bed and returned to my own. Vanessa was there still, flipping through her magazine and paying little attention to anything at all. I laid down next to her and pressed my face against the skin of her arm. I inhaled and smelled all those wonderful female smells, the cleanness and the perfume and soap, and I inhaled again and again.

What're you doing? she said.

Remembering, I said.

For a while I fell asleep and dreamed I was back in the Best Western. I think I was eating some Popeye's fried chicken out of a box and mashed potatoes from a Styrofoam cup. The TV was on, but I couldn't watch anything. The dream went on like that for a very long time, it seemed, and I just remember thinking to myself, how'd I get back here? What am I doing? And, just as I was thinking that, Vanessa woke me up. She was climbing atop me and reaching into my pajama bottoms. When I opened my eyes there she was, her hair cascading over my eyes, her breath ragged.

I missed you, I said, still half-asleep.

Instead of answering she just continued. I kept trying to speak up, saying this and that about having regretted everything I'd done and all the harm I'd caused, but regardless, I couldn't get her to answer. Vanessa was too busy with the act, with pawing and gripping at me, pushing her face into my shoulder and moaning and sobbing interchangeably. I moved my hands up and down her soft body, looking for an appropriate place to rest them. I leaned up, in the dark, and did the only thing I could think of doing. I took her ear into my mouth and gently tugged on it with my teeth. I did what I had done so many times before.

THE NEXT DAY I was sick with worry as I walked to Mackenzie's apartment. I thought of early on in the relationship, the first few times I'd skulked over there in the middle of the night, and how nervous and aroused I'd been. I had practically been shaking when she answered her door with a smile so lovely that it terrified me. We sat on her futon in the living room and listened to records for over an hour before I worked up the courage to lean in and get that first and fateful kiss. Within fifteen minutes we were fumbling toward the back bedroom and stripping each other of our clothes and mashing our mouths and lips together as we fell into the sheets.

The memory was enough to shake me. I reached to knock, but couldn't make myself follow through. Again, it was August and the summer heat bled into me and caused a manic sweat to break out. The plan that had seemed so simple the previous night—say hello, tell her the affair was concluded and that I was giving things with Vanessa another go, wish her luck and love and happiness, and say goodbye—had all but unwound completely. I didn't know if I could do it anymore, if I could say goodbye to one of the few people I'd ever loved and lusted after, and I thought of alternatives, of writing a letter like an old-fashioned coward and slipping it into her mailbox, or calling when I knew she'd be out and leaving a cropped and impersonal message. I was navigating these possibilities, searching for some kind of method, when the door opened.

Standing there, looking out, was my Mackenzie. She smiled at me, but it was less the smile I'd grown used to and more of a mischievous glare. To my surprise she was wearing her puffy winter coat with a fur-lined hood. It took a moment to remember again that I'd found myself on her doorstep in the throes of August and not December or January.

I tried to begin my plan, to say hello and then goodbye, but all I could manage was, It's nearly a hundred degrees out.

No, it's not, she said. It's freezing. Freezing cold. You're out of your mind.

She let me in then and pointed at the window A/C unit that sat just behind the futon where we'd shared our first kiss. The plastic frame was lying on the floor and the wires were sticking out like wild hairs. Next to the frame was a grab-bag assortment of screwdrivers and hammers.

Your air-conditioner went out? I said.

Uh huh, Mackenzie said, wiping a thick bead of sweat from her brow. Trying a little bit of the ol' reverse psychology to help the situation.

It was typical Mackenzie. She was a child of whimsy, a delightful cocktail of fancy and disorder that filled my cup when it'd run over with cynicism. She dressed differently, relying on hand-me-down sweaters and blouses, and accumulated piercings and hair colorings whenever it pleased her to do so. That winter, when I'd first met her and gone to her apartment to listen to music, she'd constructed a family of snow-people outside her door and dressed them in her winter clothes. That puffy jacket she was wearing had been thrown around the shoulders of the smallest one, the child of the family, I suppose. I'd asked her why and, with a shrug and a smile, she'd told me that children were our future.

Do you want me to take a look it? I asked, pointing at the air conditioner.

Knock yourself out, she said. I'm just going to sit over here and enjoy some hot chocolate.

And I'll be damned if she didn't. She sat right there on her futon and held a steaming cup in her mittened hands. I took off my coat and rolled up the sleeves of my shirt and got to work. I didn't know the first thing about air conditioners, not really anyway, but I got down there on my knees and messed with the wires and tried everything I could think of. I'd do this or that, but nothing ever happened when I hit the power button.

That's okay, she said, finishing her mug. You gave it your best shot.

I said I was sorry and went into the kitchen and got a glass of water. The cup I grabbed from the cabinets had Alvin from Alvin and the Chipmunks on the side. I guzzled down that water and tried my best to cool off. It was eighty degrees in that apartment, though, and I couldn't get my breath.

Let's go somewhere, I said. It's awful in here.

You sure? she said. I hear it's going to sleet today.

Through the window by the door I saw a couple walking down the sidewalk hand-in-hand. They were dressed in thin undershirts and shorts and sandals. In the distance the air crackled with humidity. Then, looking back to Mackenzie, I saw her sitting there on that futon, huddled up and play-shivering, looking just as happy as could be.

You're a funny gal, I said.

You think so? she said.

I do. I walked over to the futon and sat down like I had that first night. Mackenzie nuzzled into my shoulder and then came near to my face. I thought of what I'd come there to do, how I'd meant to see her in the doorway and tell her that things were over between us, but in the moment I couldn't help it. She looked so cute then, so magical, that I leaned in and kissed her as soft as I could manage.

Hey, she said, afterward. You want to get in some long-johns and hop into bed?

Tempting, I said. Maybe we should go out, though. Find a place where the air's not boiling.

Mackenzie shed her winter coat and ran her hands through her sweaty mop of hair. Don't know what you're talking about, she said, walking over and grabbing her keys off a kitchen counter.

★

WHENEVER MACKENZIE and I weren't out running around with her hedonistic friends or making love, we went to this art theater downtown. It was a wonderful little place, and wonderfully air-conditioned, so we snuck in some bottles of booze and camped out in the back row. The movie itself wasn't anything too special. One of those indie numbers. A cheaply made short film with a lot of symbolism and tons of unsigned artists providing the soundtrack. The story concerned this young, beautiful couple who were running away from their families. There was no end to the scenes where they drove through the countryside, saying nothing and listening to moment-appropriate songs. I don't think Mackenzie or I really appreciated the movie, but we held each other there in the theater and took turns drawing off our bootlegged hooch.

When the credits rolled we returned to the heat and the setting sun, drunk and happy. Nearby was this cafe that a few of Mackenzie's friends owned and operated, so we got a table on the porch and ate sandwiches and drank homemade wine. The temperature was letting off a little bit, and it was comfortable enough that we weren't sweating or cursing the weather.

At one point I said, This is nice.

It is nice, Mackenzie said. The very definition of nice.

That's exactly what I was just thinking, I said.

You know what they say, she said between bites. Great minds, etcetera, etcetera, etcetera, ad nauseam.

I laughed hard when she said that. I couldn't help it. She was the funniest girl I'd ever come across. I'd spent so long at that point trying to distance myself from her and solve the Vanessa problem that I'd lost sight of that fact. I was reminded, though, that August day, how much I truly adored that girl, and I started remembering the fantasies I'd carried around for so long then, of the two of us moving to the country somewhere and raising beautiful children of our own in a home filled with music and art. I thought of her standing at the altar, a picture of beauty and health and free-spiritedness, a daisy poetically tucked behind an ear or woven into her long hair.

Well then, I said, can you guess what I'm thinking about now?

She took a drink of her water and grinned. Was it about how you came over to end things with us?

I tried to deny it, to pretend like that'd never been the case, but couldn't.

I haven't heard from you in over a week, she said. And for the last two months you've been showing up in wrinkled clothes and smelling like booze and a hotel. You think I can't figure out where you slept last night?

It seemed I was caught red-handed. There was no explanation, no alibi or manufactured story to offer. I told her I was going to say goodbye today.

That's what I figured. That's what I figured was going to happen all along anyway.

Really? I said. It's been that obvious?

Mackenzie drank her water again and turned her plate on the table. Someone nearby said something into a phone and a car honked its horn. He always goes back to his wife, she said. It's a story as old as time. Everybody knows it, if they're being honest with themselves.

Huh, I said.

Huh, she said.

Right then I did the only thing I knew to do. I reached across the table and grabbed her hand. I rubbed the pad of my thumb over her skin and knuckles and wrist and looked at her. You know I love you, I said.

I know, she said.

One of the friends who owned the restaurant came out onto the porch then and talked to us. Her hair was strange, in that half of her head was shaved and the other spiked like a mohawk. She and Mackenzie discussed something that'd happened at a bar the night before. They laughed, both of them did, but Mackenzie's looked forced. Every time her face lit up, I could tell it was masking tragedy. I wanted to interrupt, to ask if she wanted to take off right then, like that couple in the movie, and head west to some new town and new life. I had enough money that we could've made it a good ways, maybe found some hotel like the Best Western and hunkered down until we found work. Then maybe we could have the house in the country, the kids, rooms full of songs and love.

I didn't, though. I got to thinking about Vanessa and Bradley, the two of them probably sitting in the dining room right then, picking over their cooling food, and it stopped the proposal dead in my throat. Instead, I paid for the sandwiches and the wine and drove Mackenzie back to her apartment.

We got to the doorway and I tried to say my

goodbyes. I kept telling her that I loved her, that I cared more than she'd ever know, and then I'd turn to leave but just stand there. At one point she was crying, and I was crying, too. She asked if I wanted to come inside and clean up and I did just that. In the bathroom she dabbed my face with a washrag and made sad attempts at jokes. Then I told her she'd make a beautiful mother someday, and the both of us sobbed.

We went into the living room again, and I looked at the winter coat draped over the arm of the futon and the air conditioner with its guts spilled all over the floor. She sat down, and I sat down next to her. There wasn't music, not really a sound at all save for the neighboring apartments and their tenants milling about, but it felt then just as it had that first night, like the world was bursting forth with new opportunities. She kissed me this time and I kissed her back. We hummed a song that'd played that first night, a sad little tune. I told her how I wished I could have it all, how I wanted her and Vanessa and Bradley, and she stroked my hair and brought me in close to her chest.

I laid my head there, and I thought for a good long time. For some reason I remembered my mother, too, standing in the kitchen in the house I grew up in, and the way her hands smelled like dish soap and steaming hot water. You're growing up, she'd said, patting my cheek and turning her head adoringly. There're things you're going to have to do, she'd said.

I thought about that and Vanessa and my boy. From where I was I could hear Mackenzie's heart quickening and then slowing. It made a shoosh in my ear. Shoosh. Shoosh. Shoosh. And then something happened. I felt the tip of my thumb breeching my lips and heading for the roof of my mouth. I let it. And then, I simply closed my eyes and let everything flow around me.

✪ VOLCANO ✪

I'M PRYING OFF my boots when my wife Brenda tells me what my fourteen-year-old daughter's principal told her this afternoon. There's an abandoned house on Wilkshire, she says to me. Apparently a bunch of kids have been going over there after school. They got caught yesterday and Wendy's name popped up.

Popped up, I say. What does pop up mean?

Well, my wife says, according to Mr. Stewart, she's the main attraction.

I have to ask her again just to understand what we're talking about.

While she tells me one more time what that means I've got my head in my hands. One of my boots sits on the floor and the other is still hanging off my foot. I don't have the energy to pull it off.

How many boys? I say. How old?

Plenty, she says. Younger ones and older ones.

Anyone we know? I say.

Jeff next door, she says. I guess he's one of them.

It takes everything I have not to march next door and drag Jeff out of his house and beat him to death in the street. Son of a bitch, I say.

My wife is calmer than me. Always has been. She's the kind who hears the smoke alarm in the middle of the night and has the wherewithal to say it might just be the batteries. As I sit there breathing hard she pulls out the chair next to mine and rubs my back. It's going to be all right, she says softly into my ear. This is going to be all right.

I'm listening, but I'm also picturing Wendy, but not as she is now. Back when she was seven years old, when she had braces on her teeth and ribbons in her hair. We used to play with dinosaurs and color in her dinosaur coloring books. We mixed baking soda and vinegar and pretended it was a volcano.

Jesus christ, I say. What do we do?

My wife kneads my shoulder now and shakes her head. I guess we talk to her, she says. We wait and when she gets here we talk.

Jesus christ, I say again.

I know, my wife says.

An hour and a half later the front door opens and in walks Wendy. She's been at play practice, or at least that's where she says she's been. Already I'm having a hard time separating Wendy Before Today and Wendy Now.

Why don't you come sit down? my wife says to her, patting a cushion on the couch.

What's going on? Wendy says, setting her backpack down by the coat closet. You guys okay? Dad looks sick.

I am sick, I say without thinking.

Come sit down, my wife says.

Wendy sits down on the couch, but not on the cushion my wife patted. Instead she retreats to the arm farthest from us. I look at her and then catch myself searching her neck for bruises. She's wearing a tank top and a tight pair of jeans. Before we even say anything I want to order her upstairs to put something else on.

I had a talk with Mr. Stewart, my wife says to her.

Wendy sighs in a manner that she's only started sighing recently. It's a sigh that says she'd rather be anywhere else than sitting there and talking with us. And what'd he have to say? she says.

Well, my wife says, he brought up an issue we need to discuss.

Then all of the color in Wendy's cheeks run out. She is suddenly pale and melting into our cream-colored sectional. Okay, she says.

Do you want to tell us what's been going on? my wife says, obviously trying to keep her voice measured. Do you want to tell us about the boys? she says.

What boys? Wendy says.

The fucking boys, I say, unable to stop myself. Tell us about the fucking boys.

WE SIGN UP for a conference with the principal Mr. Stewart and the guidance counselor Ms. Taylor. It's two days after we found out about the boys and the house on Wilkshire, and we shuffle into Mr. Stewart's office in the middle school. The school itself is exactly how I pictured it. The hallways are coated in posters that say WHAT DO YOU WANT TO BE? and MAKE TODAY EVEN BETTER THAN YESTERDAY. One that hangs over the main office's doorway is silver with glittered blue letters and reads GO PANTHERS. As we walk in I want to tear it down and rip it to shreds.

Mr. Stewart's office is decorated with old pictures of the middle school throughout the years. You can see it growing and modernizing as you look from frame to frame. It starts as a small building and then doubles and triples in size. On Mr. Stewart's desk is a plate with his name embossed in the same blue letters as the sign leading in. Brenda and me sit across from Mr. Stewart, who sits behind his desk in a leather chair.

Ms. Taylor will be right with us, he says and smiles.

Sure, my wife says.

Ms. Taylor's new, Mr. Stewart says, but she's a great counselor already.

Oh, my wife says. That's great.

It is, Mr. Stewart says. He swivels in his chair and opens a drawer in his desk. He looks inside and then closes it. He's bald except for a path of hair on the top and a ring around the sides. His teeth are needle-like and yellowed. She graduated from Indiana State, he says. They have a very good program.

Just as he's done saying this in comes Ms. Taylor. She's twenty-three, maybe twenty-four, her blonde hair cut short and fashionable. I'm sorry, she says. Traffic was bad this morning.

Sure, I say, knowing that traffic wasn't bad on our way in.

72

All right, Mr. Stewart says, now that we've got everyone here we can start. Ms. Taylor, would you like to fill in the parents on what's going on?

We know, my wife says. I can tell she doesn't want to hear it again. Our meeting, Mr. Stewart, she says, was sufficient.

Sure, Mr. Stewart says. Good, he says.

Well, Ms. Taylor says, there have been some developments.

Developments? I say.

Ms. Taylor, Mr. Stewart says, had a visit yesterday from the mother of another student.

A friend of Wendy's, Ms. Taylor says. Her mother came by and let me know what had happened.

What happened? my wife says.

One of Wendy's classmates, Mr. Stewart says, was recently found to be pregnant.

I can't help it. My hand goes to my face.

She's three months along, Ms. Taylor says.

Oh god, my wife says.

What the hell is going on around here? I say.

Just what does that mean? Mr. Stewart says.

Now, Ms. Taylor says.

No, Mr. Stewart says. From where I'm sitting, you don't have any room to come in here and make comments like that.

And just what does that mean? I say.

Ms. Taylor sits down in the chair next my wife and me and says, Let's all calm down.

I agree, Mr. Stewart says and takes a deep breath. There's no need to get all up in arms.

Seems like there's a lot of reason, I say. And then, I

need someone to tell me something. I need to hear exactly what this whole mess is about.

It's been going on for a while now, Ms. Taylor says, turning to my wife and me. She looks sad, a little scared. Groups of students have been hanging around this old house on Wilkshire, she says. Over by the post office.

I've seen it, I say, picturing the crumbling house I pass sometimes on my way to work. It's the one with the green siding that's coming off.

That's right, Ms. Taylor says. So, they've been going over there maybe a year, maybe a year and a half. And most of the time they drink and smoke pot and things like that.

Things like that? my wife says.

Ms. Taylor puts her hands out, as if she's trying to stop an oncoming car. I mean, it's just been juvenile delinquent-type behavior. Nothing too crazy.

Ms. Taylor, Mr. Stewart says and coughs.

What I'm trying to say, she says, is that all of that changed about six months ago. The boys brought some girls over to the house and they did some, uh, things.

Things, I say, knowing exactly what things means.

Wendy was one of them, Ms. Taylor says. She was a regular over there.

What Ms. Taylor is trying to say, Mr. Stewart says, leaning on his elbows on his desk, is that you should get Wendy to a doctor.

What for? my wife says.

Get her checked out, Mr. Stewart says. See what we're dealing with here and then we'll deal with it.

74

★

I TAKE A FEW DAYS off work while everything gets figured out. In the evening, while Wendy holes up in her bedroom and cries, my wife sits at the kitchen table and flips through photo albums. She pays the most attention to the one she's kept of Wendy through the years. She says, Hey, come over here, and holds up a Polaroid of Wendy, two years old, shoving her face into a paper plate of ice cream.

You remember this one? she says.

Sure, I say.

You need to try and not be mad, she says to me.

I'm not mad, I lie.

The only time we see Wendy is when she comes out to use the bathroom or to grab food. She hasn't eaten much since this whole thing broke. Maybe a handful of chips and an apple or two. When she comes through tonight she's getting a glass of water from the sink. She's wearing a black t-shirt and a pair of black basketball shorts.

Hi honey, my wife says to no response. How you feeling?

Wendy stops in the kitchen and looks at my wife and then me. She bats her eyes, like she's sending Morse Code, like she's spelling out FUCK and YOU with her eyelashes, and then retreats to her bedroom again.

This is goddamn awful, I say when she slams the door behind her.

My wife has stopped reassuring me. Instead, she searches through the photo album until she finds another picture, this one of Wendy on a trip to the fire station in the first grade. She's wearing a plastic fireman's helmet and giving the camera a thumbs-up with her tiny thumb.

What happened? my wife says, asking no one but herself.

In the morning she gets up and showers and dresses for the doctor's appointment. Wendy doesn't bother and only changes out of her basketball shorts and into a pair of jeans. As they're walking out the door I go to hug her out of reflex. Both of us recoil.

You sure you don't want me to go? I ask my wife.

No, she says. It's all right.

Okay, I say, and watch them get into our car and drive away.

As soon as they've disappeared around the corner I go into Wendy's room. I've been planning this since yesterday. Last night I laid in bed and imagined myself doing it, but couldn't think of anything I really wanted to uncover.

Luckily I don't come across anything terrible. Some notes from her friends. School pictures. A stash of about seventy dollars. But what I do find is a notebook with the words SECRET written on the cover. I take it and plop down on Wendy's bed. I flip through the pages and see it's nothing but newly-drawn doodles. Some of them are of birds with strange faces, people with beehive hairdos, some robots. Toward the middle though, I see a series of drawings that make my chest feel tight. They're of dinosaurs, like the ones she used to draw.

What're you doing there? I'd say to her back then.

She'd be sitting at her table, leaning over and trying

to hide what she was drawing. Nothing, she'd say.

I'd say, I think you're drawing dinosaurs, and try and catch a peek.

No, she'd say. No, I'm not drawing any dinosaurs. You're crazy.

I look through the doodles on her bed. There're all the dinosaurs we used to draw and play with. The Tyrannosauruses, Stegosauruses, Triceratopses. I laugh whenever I turn the page to a new kind and remember the names.

Back when she was little I'd asked her what her favorite dinosaur was. Brontosaurus was always her answer.

Why's that? I asked.

Because, she said, scribbling with a Crayon, they're the biggest of the big and they could hurt everyone, but they don't hurt no one.

I stop in the tablet on a picture of a brontosaurus. It's a pretty good drawing, all things considered. He's half-submerged in a prehistoric swamp, his long, thin neck reaching up and out of the water. He's got a bowtie on about three-quarters of the way up and a big, dumb grin on his face.

That's all I can handle. I put the tablet back where I found it and pace from her room to the kitchen to the living room and then outside. I can't stop moving. Finally I decide to put all that energy to use. I clean the kitchen, scrub the bathroom floor, vacuum the carpet. When that's done I put on my work boots and head to the garage. I grab one of my gas cans off the bench out there and gas up my mower. After making quick work of the yard, I stand there looking at my house like I'm a stranger, like I've never been inside.

I'm out there thinking about everything, about Wendy, about how time moves the way it does, and I see something out of the corner of my eye. It's next door. And then I see it's Jeff peeking out the front window. When he sees that I see him he jumps away quick, lets the curtain fall back in place. For the briefest of moments I consider going over there and kicking in the door.

Back when Wendy was coloring dinosaurs, Jeff was her best friend. Came to all of her birthday parties, was usually the only boy there. Sometimes there'd be other ones, but when they got too rough, like boys get, he was always the one who stood up for her, who protected her.

Seeing Jeff seals the deal for me. I go into the garage again and grab a couple of the gas cans. I don't even bother putting up the mower. I get in my truck and head for town. I can see out of my side mirror that Jeff's back at the window, watching me go.

Halfway there my cell rings. I look at the screen and it says my wife's name. At first I reach to answer it, but then I realize I don't want to hear what she has to say. I let it go to voicemail and then the next notice appears.

1 UNHEARD MESSAGE.

Hanging there like a bad omen.

On Wilkshire I pull into the driveway of the old house. There are beer cans and bottles strewn about, fast food wrappers. A condom here and there. The house sits like a bad tooth. Gray and rotting. The inside isn't any better. Mold-lined walls. Sagging floors. Junk and magazines and water-logged cigarette butts in piles. For a second I try and imagine Wendy here and can't help but shake.

To start I splash the front room with gas from both of my cans and lay it on thick even though a place like this would go up like a box of matches if you just gave it half the chance. Just to be sure though, I lay a line of gas from the front door to the exposed main line in what must have been the utility closet.

Outside I get a lighter out of the back of my truck, one of those long ones you use for hot water heaters. I spark it and look at the flame. It's tiny and what little breeze there is sends it dancing. Before I touch it to the line of gas, I'm back to thinking about Wendy again, young Wendy, smashing her dinosaurs together on the table. I'm remembering pouring the vinegar into the baking soda and watching it bubble.

A volcano, she'd squeal.

And why did all the volcanoes go off? I'd say.

Back then? she'd say.

Back then, I'd say. Back when all the dinosaurs were around.

She'd stop for a moment. She'd put all of herself into that question. Because, she'd say.

Because why?

Because, she'd say, we had to get our chance too.

That's right, I'd tell her. That's exactly right.

✪ BEAR FIGHT ✪

MY OLD GRANDDAD was the meanest sonuvabitch in Greene County, Indiana, and anybody tells you different doesn't know their dick from a hole in the ground. Now that's the truth. That man used to work the mine every day and then get home and sit in the backyard and shoot his pistol in the air. Damndest thing you've ever seen. He'd be out there with a jug of wine and his peacekeeper all night until Grandma drug him back in. Harry, she'd say, there ain't no daylight left. He'd fire one last shot off and grab his jug. I seen it a hundred times if I saw it once.

Anyway, Granddad used to tell stories about his buddies from way back. Most of 'em were about how they ran around with ladies who weren't their wives and drank all night and smoked and talked bullshit. He had him a buddy named Gary that fought a bear once. I ain't lying to you. They used to have these shows at the armory where fellas brought in bears and whoever was dumb enough to think they could fight those 'em signed up on a sheet and got in a cage. That bear was muzzled, of course, but it was mean. If you could stay on your feet five full minutes you got a prize.

Let's say twenty dollars. Maybe thirty.

Way Granddad told the story him and the boys went to see the fights and got them a seat in the bleachers. Bunch of people went in there to fight bears and the rest came to bet on the fighting. I got that fella right there going a minute, they'd say, and pony up the cash. Anyway, somebody snuck in some whiskey and Granddad and his buddies passed it around and watched. Nobody could last much longer than a few seconds. They'd get in there in that cage and that bear would take a swipe and knock 'em on their ass. The guy that owned that bear would jump in between long enough to let the unlucky fella go running out the cage.

Granddad and his buddies were drinking whiskey and laughing up a storm. That's the way he told it. Then one of his buddies, this fella named Clarke, talked another one of 'em into giving it a go. Clarke was something of a shit-starter. He was always chesting up on guys and giving them the what-for. And if he wasn't looking for a fight he was getting in your head and riling you up enough to fight somebody else. That night he was in Gary's ear.

Gary was something of an idiot, but big and strong as a blue-ribbon ox. That's what Granddad always said. A blue-ribbon ox. Said he used to be able to lift the back-end of a pick-up off the ground. Just like that. Like it was nothing.

Hey Gary, Clarke said in the stands, that bear don't look like much.

Granddad said he looked at Gary and saw Gary looking at the bear. He had his head cocked, I guess. He was squinting his eyes, I guess. He was sizing up that bear.

Hey Gary, Clarke said, get in there and give that bear a go. Us boys could use a good laugh.

Most of the time Clarke would lay into Gary about this thing or that, whether it was the questionable breeding of his folks or how he couldn't hardly tie his shoes, until he'd get so steamed Gary'd have to walk away or Granddad or one of the other fellas had to tell him to knock it off. Gary was a sweetheart, that's how Grandma put it, she said he couldn't of hurt a fly. Whenever she'd lay that on Granddad would whistle like she didn't know what she was talking about and then crack his knuckles and start in on this story.

He'd say, That's when Gary got up off the seat and walked down toward the cage. There was another fella in there getting his. That bear was tossing this poor son-of-a-gun from post to post. He said he tried to talk Gary out of it but Gary was already signed up.

Gary got in that cage and the handler gave him some instructions. That bear——and Granddad said he stood at least eight feet tall, weighed something like half a ton——was up on his hind legs and stalking over to Gary. It was growling from under its muzzle and Granddad said there was spit running all over the place.

Now listen to this. You're likely not gonna believe this, but Gary got in that cage with that bear and held his own. Here was the trick – he got in close. He waited for that bear to take a swipe with one of his paws and he ducked his way in by its chest. Granddad said he gave that bear a couple of jabs in the ribs, even got one into its muzzled chin. The bear was beating Gary's back with its paws and claws but he just wrapped his big arms around the bear's waist and held on.

There was a scoreboard on the wall of the armory that kept time for JV basketball games and it ticked down how long the fighters had been in the cage. Gary managed to hold onto that bastard until there was something like twenty seconds left. Then the bear fell on its back and Gary hit the floor. The scoreboard buzzer went off and the place went nuts.

Gary was beat to hell, his back covered in cuts and blood and it swelled up and turned black and blue for the better part of a month. Granddad and the boys carried him out of the armory and into one of the bars they liked to drink at and promptly got good and fucked. He said Gary didn't pay for a beer for a long, long time after that.

Ain't that the damndest thing you ever heard? A man fighting a bear? Granddad swore up and down it was true. Got out a bible one time. Yeah, I mean he got a bible down from the bookshelf and put his hand right on there. Said I swear to God above that shit happened. Swear it on everything good in this here goddamn world.

But every time he told that story he couldn't help but get into what happened later. I mean, much later. Fifteen, sixteen years. This was after the group of guys stopped pal-ing around so much. After Granddad quit drinking and shooting in the backyard. He settled down and started playing rummy with Grandma instead of raising hell and running.

He said it got to the point that him and the fellas got together maybe once a year. They'd hold a party or something for Christmas or a birthday or if somebody kicked the bucket. People got families, he said, they got other things to worry about. But I guess one of those times they headed over to Gary's house. He had himself a wife by then and a little place out by where the drive-in used to be. It wasn't long after he and that woman bought that house that he invited Granddad and Clarke and the rest of the crowd over to give them a tour.

Granddad said Gary took them in the back and showed them where his wife was going to plant a garden and where he was going to build himself a tool shed. He got out a bag of grass seed and pitched some out while everyone watched. He took them upstairs and showed them the bedrooms and the bathrooms and pointed out where he'd already fixed a few things. Got them in the kitchen and his wife made everybody a drink.

The way I heard it, seems like Gary's woman wasn't the prettiest gal. Apparently she had thinning hair and a mouthful of teeth going this way and that. Granddad said her eyes were a little off, like in a way you couldn't exactly tell exactly where she was looking. But I guess she was a genuine sweetheart. She doted on Gary and Granddad and all the fellas, made sure they always had drinks and snacks.

Honey, she said to Gary at one point, take the boys downstairs and show them the basement. Show them the TV and the fryer we just bought.

So Gary did that. He led the fellas downstairs.

Here's the TV, he said to them and pointed at the

set in the corner. That's an RCA.

Mighty fine set, somebody said.

The best, my granddad said.

And here's the fryer, Gary said and pointed to a counter by the stairs where an electric fry basket was plugged in. She can't stop talking about it, he said and motioned upstairs. For some reason all she ever wanted in her life was to own a fryer.

Gary plugged the thing in and before too long the oil was bubbling and the whole basement smelled of grease. He opened a freezer nearby and got out a bag of frozen fries and poured them in. Then he showed the fellas the other parts of the basement, some of the things he'd fixed.

Clarke wasn't too impressed though. Apparently he'd been in a shit mood the whole time. Granddad said he had his hands shoved in his pockets by the TV. He said, You ought to save your money. He said, Maybe spend some dough on getting that wife of yours some new teeth.

Granddad said Gary didn't move at first. Clarke was laughing a bit to himself like it was supposed to be some kind of joke. When he looked at Granddad to see if he was going to laugh Granddad said all he saw was Gary walking over to where Clarke was standing by the TV. He had the basket of that fryer in hand and he slung a cloud of white-hot grease at Clarke's face.

It hit him flush.

The next thing that happened was that Clarke fell to the ground and screamed and kicked. Granddad said you could smell him burning, smell him cooking. The fellas all got down with him and one of them slung their jacket over his head. Someone else ran upstairs and called an ambulance. Ten minutes later and an EMT carried Clarke out on a stretcher, gauze wrapped around his still bubbling face.

Gary didn't move from where he'd pitched the grease at Clarke. He still held the basket in his hand. When everyone ran off to go home or to the hospital, he stood there in the spot, just staring at his feet. Granddad stayed with him until the police came and led him out in cuffs. Said that was the last he really saw of either one of them. Clarke moved off to be tended to by family and Gary went away awhile.

Granddad would tell that story and Grandma would shake her head and say, These things happen. That didn't seem to make Granddad feel any better. He'd look at his hands like he was looking for some kind of answer, but it never came. Instead, he'd start talking about that bear all over again and say something like, Eight feet tall. Or, Half a ton. I'll swear on a bible, he'd say. Go and get one off the shelf. I'll swear right here in front of God and law and country. You may not believe it, he'd say, but you would if you seen it. Anything can happen. Anything at all.

THAT'S HOW
✪ A MAN LIVES ✪

MY LANDLORD stopped by a little after two in the afternoon. I knew what he was there for. He'd called the day before and told me he wanted to talk to me about the cats. He said he'd heard from a maintenance fella I had three cats in the house when the lease said I could only have one. Truth was that I had four cats. They kept coming around my porch and I kept feeding them. Before I knew it they were inside and settling in.

He knocked on the door, my landlord did. He was a little guy who looked like he'd been melted down from a bigger guy. All sorts of loose skin. A sad face. Sometimes he wore a half-undone Christmas tie in April. Sanders, he said through the door, you home?

There wasn't much I could do but answer the door. The house was a wreck. Didn't matter if I ran around or tried to give it a quick clean. It'd really gone to the dogs at that point. Or, I guess, the cats. There were litter boxes everywhere and food spilled on the floor. There wasn't even much use in trying to gather up all the cats and hide them either. If I shoved them all in a room my landlord was gonna hear them singing and crying.

Hey, I said to him. How you doing, Brad?

God, he said. Sanders, I just don't know anymore.

You or me either, I said and held the door open for him to come in.

Brad plopped down on the couch in my living room. There were a pair of cats sleeping there. One was on the armrest opposite where Brad was sitting and the other was snoozing on the back. Brad slapped his knees a couple of times and whistled. I guess you know why I'm over here, he said.

Sure, I said. Doesn't take a scientist.

He said, No, it does not, and petted the cat on the back of the couch. She was a white cat with matted fur and crust in her eyes. At first she let him pet her and then she realized what was happening and batted at his hand and gave him a hiss. That was her game. She ain't very friendly, is she? Brad said.

Nah, I said. She knows what she wants.

We should all be so lucky, Brad said. He pointed at the TV. It was turned to some golf. There was a man wearing an orange shirt and orange hat standing in a fairway. He was looking at something far away and the announcer said, I think he's got it now. You a golfer? Brad asked me.

Used to be, I said and finally took a seat in my old recliner next to the couch. When I did a cloud of cat hair jumped out of the cushions and fell through the air. Me and my buddies used to get a six-pack apiece and just go out to the club and hack around.

That's the life, Brad said. Say, he said, how many cats you got anyway?

I looked to the entrance into the kitchen and saw another cat walking in. He was a tom I liked to call Gray because of his dull, gray coat. Him and the other tom of the house--he didn't have a name--were all the time fighting over the females. But neither of the females really wanted anything to do with them. All they had to show for it at the end of the day was a bunch of fresh scars and some patches of missing hair.

Four, I said. Brad, I've got four cats in here. Not even gonna try and bullshit you. It's not like I went out looking to own four cats. It's not like I went out on that porch and shook a bag of food and waited for them to come running. It just happened, I said. I don't know. I guess they found me.

Gray made its way over to where Brad was sitting and rubbed his head against Brad's shin. Brad leaned down and gave him a scratch between the eyes. I think he likes me, he said.

I didn't have the heart to tell him it was marking its territory.

Whatever happened to that sweet little girl who moved in here with you? he said.

Long gone, I said. Met a woman in her therapy group.

No shit, he said. I liked her.

Me too, I said and went to scratch my nose. There was hair all over my fingers.

I knew right then I should've just apologized for the cats and ask what he'd like me to do about it, but

89

instead I asked him how things were on his end.

How're the kids? I said. How's Vera?

Oh god, he said. I just don't know anymore.

Don't know anymore? I said.

The kids, he said, they're a mess. The boy doesn't want to go to school. All he wants to do is lay in bed all day and get high out in the garage. I caught him in there the other day with his pants unzipped and a doobie smoking next to him in an ashtray. What do you say to that?

I'm not sure, I said.

Me either, Brad said. There's no book telling people how to prepare for that. And the girl, she's no better. She's got her a couple of boyfriends around town. Hardly ever comes home and when she does it's only for a shower and a meal.

Brad, I said, I'm sorry.

It's fine, he said and touched the white cat again. This time she moved into his petting and purred so loudly I could hear her from where I was sitting. And Vera, he said. Vera's just a piece of work.

I'd met her a few times and knew that to be the case. Once she brought me over a tin of cookies at the end of November. They were Christmas cookies and they weren't bad. She was obsessed with the holiday though. Every time I saw her she was wearing earrings shaped like trees or bells or holly. Sweaters with snowmen and the like. That'd helped me make sense of Brad and his Christmas tie and why he'd wear sometimes in the spring.

Did you know, he said, that we keep a tree up year round?

90

Year round? I said. I didn't know that.

January to December, he said. While everyone's out in the street setting off fireworks or cooking hot dogs in their backyards, we're sitting there in that goddamn living room looking at that goddamn Christmas tree.

I said, How about that?

How about that? he said. How about that? And you know what? It started slow. At first she just wanted to put it up right after Thanksgiving and then take it down after New Year's. That was fine. There was no problem with that. No argument to be had. But then New Year's stretched into February. That's where I was gonna draw the line, Sanders. I said there's no way that tree's gonna see Valentine's Day. And do you know what happened?

I'm guessing it saw Valentine's Day.

That's right, he said. You got it. Then March. Then April. So on and so on.

I shook my head. There wasn't much I could say or add. The gray tom came over and jumped up in my lap. He scratched my thigh with his claws and I kicked him off onto the floor.

Say, Brad said, wiping a line of sweat from his forehead, you wouldn't have a beer would you?

Sure, I said. If there was one thing I had besides cats back then it was beer.

I gave him one and he opened it and had a drink. The white cat got mad at him again and jumped down off the couch and walked around. Thanks, he said and lifted the can. I'm not meaning to get worked up here. I didn't mean to come over here and interrupt whatever it was you had going.

Hey, I said, motioning at the golf on the TV and the

cats all over the place. You're looking at everything I had going.

It's not bad, he said. Few more cats than I'd prefer, but that's how a man lives. He does what he has to do.

I guess that's right, I said and watched the second tom making its way through the kitchen, stretching and yawning.

Brad said, We got a garage full of decorations, but it was like he wasn't talking to me anymore. It's all crammed in there so tight, he said, that I can't even park the truck in there anymore.

That's a shame, I said and looked at the TV. The golfer in the orange shirt and orange hat was lining up a putt. You need another one? I asked Brad.

Sure, he said and put the empty can on the floor. I'll take another one. Keep 'em coming. You care if I stick around a short? he said, getting comfortable. Don't feel like going home right yet. I can see why all these critters come round.

You got it, I said, making my way through a floor's worth of cats and into the kitchen.

YOU HAVE TO
✪ HAVE SOMEBODY ✪

AFTER THE MOVIE the couples split up and took separate cars back to Kerry and Aileen's house. Aileen rode with Mary Ann and Mary Ann's husband Rick rode shotgun with Kerry. The men passed the remnants of a travel-sized bottle of Early Times Kerry had snuck into the movie back and forth and took their turns finishing it off.

I tell you, Kerry said between sips, Aileen and me couldn't be happier that you two came around. This town was as dull as could be before you got here.

Is that right? Rick said and took the bottle back. Cause Mary Ann and me are just as happy that we found you two.

Kerry turned onto the street he and Aileen lived on and told Rick about the last couple the two of them had been friends with. You never saw people that dull, he said. All they wanted to do was sit around and talk politics and food drives.

Shit gets old, Rick said. Hey, they beat us here.

You guys, Aileen said from the driveway, drive slower than a carfull of old folks.

Better old folks than being a couple of law-breaking delinquents, Kerry said as he got out of the car.

Seriously, Aileen said. I could've walked here faster than you two drove.

They're old men, Mary Ann said and laughed.

That's right, Aileen said. We should cut these two geezers some slack.

My question, Kerry said and walked over to give Aileen a hard kiss on the mouth, is what could have possibly aged us prematurely? Perhaps a couple of shrewish wives?

Mary Ann gave Rick a punch on the shoulder. You don't say a word, she said.

I'm not saying anything, Rick said, squinting his eyes before rearing back with the empty bottle of Early Time and throwing it through the night sky and into a patch of bushes in front of a house across the street.

Good throw, Kerry said and unlocked his front door. You play outfield in high school?

Shortstop, Mary Ann answered for Rick. He played some in college too.

Ooh la la, Aileen said.

Kerry flipped on a light inside and gestured for everyone to go in. My friend here, he said and slapped Rick on the back as he walked in, is a man of mystery. I tell you, I never thought I'd have such a mysterious friend, Aileen.

It's something, she said from inside. We've got beer

in the fridge and some whiskey and rum in the pantry.

We're almost out of beer, Kerry said. My guess is we've got exactly three beers.

Two, Aileen called out.

Two, Kerry said. My guess is two beers.

We could go get some more, Mary Ann said. We'd be happy to make a run, wouldn't we Rick?

Sure thing, Rick said.

Aileen popped her head around the corner and held out a pair of nearly full bottles of liquor. I think we're going to be just fine, she said.

Liquor night, Kerry said loudly.

Honey, Aileen said. You're being loud.

So what? he answered. Honey, look around. We're among friends. We've got our friends here and they don't care a bit if I'm loud. Do you?

No sir, Mary Ann said.

This right here, Rick said, is your domicile.

Domicile, Kerry repeated. Aileen, tell me, what'd we ever do to get such funny friends?

Rick and Mary Ann and Kerry joined Aileen in the kitchen as she was pouring four juice glasses full of whiskey. Did Kerry tell you about his old friend Clarke? she said.

I was doing just that, Kerry jumped in.

That the politics and food drives fella? Rick asked.

That's the one, Aileen said. He was such a nice guy, Mary Ann, but he had nothing to offer in the way of conversation. He'd sit down at your table and you'd hand him a drink and he'd start rattling off like he was the nightly news.

Today, Kerry said with his best news anchor voice,

fourteen dead in Rwanda and another thirty dying of starvation in this very community.

Kerry, Aileen said.

Well, he said, I'm not lying am I?

No, she said, but let's not make fun.

Oh, Kerry said and crossed himself, heaven forbid. We don't want to blasphemy poor old Saint Clarke.

He's not far off, Aileen said to Mary Ann and Rick. I mean, he was just about as boring as they come. And his wife wasn't much better.

Talk about a Debbie-Downer, Kerry said and had a seat. He picked up one of the glasses of whiskey and sipped from it. What was she always going on about? She had something she was always harping about.

Vaccinations, Aileen said.

What about vaccinations? Mary Ann asked.

Oh god, Rick yelled. Vaccinations this, vaccinations that. That's right, goddamn vaccinations. She had a theory, Rick, that the government was putting shit in their vaccinations. What that shit was supposed to do, I'll never know.

She believed, Aileen continued, the government was giving people diseases with their vaccinations.

Kerry took another sip of whiskey and grimaced. I don't say this lightly, he said, and I don't mean to be mean, but she was a cuckoo bird.

Kerry, Aileen said.

But listen here, Kerry said, me and Aileen are hogging the floor. For all I know you two are going to be talking to your future friends about what motor-mouths good ol' Kerry and Aileen were.

We wouldn't do that, Rick said.

Here, Aileen said and handed Rick and Mary Ann glasses of whiskey, have a drink.

That won't happen, Mary Ann assured them before taking a sip. Do you have anything to mix this with? she said and then, I'll tell you why, too––the four of us? We're going to be friends for life.

Hear hear, Rick said and raised his glass.

Friends for life, Kerry repeated and raised his glass too.

We've got some coke, Aileen said to Mary Ann, and there's always water.

How about just a little bit of coke? Mary Ann said.

Aileen got a bottle out of the fridge. Some coke for my friend for life, she said.

Mary Ann stirred the coke into the whiskey with her index finger and had another drink. She smiled afterwards and said, That's perfect.

Aileen threw her arm around Mary Ann and kissed her on the cheek. Look at my friend for life here, she said to Kerry.

You're drunk, Kerry said.

False, Aileen said. I'm close to drunk and well on my way to full-on drunk.

This woman, Kerry said, you get her a couple of cocktails before a movie, then three sips of something during, and she's humming like a machine.

I had four sips, Aileen said.

Correction then, Kerry said. Four sips.

Say, Aileen said to Mary Ann, who was still in her grasp, we're doing all the talking. We said we were going to stop and we're still the ones talking up a storm. Tell me, she said, how did you and Rick over here meet?

Yeah, Kerry said. I don't feel like I know anything about you guys.

Well, Rick said, she was best friends with this girl I used to go out with.

There we go, Kerry said and banged his fist on the table. Now we're getting to it.

Whoa whoa, Aileen said and squeezed Mary Ann closer.

And this girl, Rick said, we shouldn't of dated in the first place.

No, Mary Ann said, you shouldn't of.

We both worked at the school, Rick said. I was teaching history back then and she was the secretary in the main office.

Wait, Kerry said. You were a teacher?

High school, Rick said and had a drink.

He was a great teacher, Mary Ann added.

Anyway, Rick said, we were dating and she shared an apartment with Mary Ann. We didn't have too much in common, this girl and me, and pretty soon I was coming around and asking Mary Ann out.

That is a story, Kerry said. Were there fireworks?

You bet, Mary Ann said. She was none too happy.

I can't imagine she was, Aileen said.

Mary Ann snuck out from Aileen's arm and took a seat at the table next to Kerry. She stirred her whiskey and coke some more and then said, We had a pretty bad falling-out, me and her.

What was her name? Kerry asked.

Audrey, Rick said.

I don't like the name Audrey, Aileen said.

You know what? Kerry said. I don't either. Fuck

Audrey, he said and lifted his glass to toast again.

Fuck Audrey, Rick said.

Mary Ann shot Rick a dirty look from where she was sitting. That's not very nice, she said. She was my friend.

Well, Aileen said, a good friend would've seen the writing on the wall and stepped aside.

Well, Mary Ann said, that didn't exactly happen in this case.

Audrey was a real bitch, Rick said.

There it is, Kerry said. The truth comes out.

Rick, Mary Ann said.

I'm just calling 'em how I see 'em, Rick said.

That's fine, she said, but you don't have to be crude about it.

My buddy here, Kerry said, is telling it like it is.

Rick smiled at Kerry and drank some whiskey. She was so pissed at us that she cost me my job. She was one of those vindictive bitches.

Lord, Aileen said, Kerry's got some stories for you.

I do, Kerry said. My god do I have some stories.

Rick, Mary Ann said.

Oh, Rick said, whatever. We're among friends.

I tell you what, Aileen said, how about we girls go have a smoke break?

Okay, Mary Ann said. I think I need one.

You two go out and gossip like a couple of hens, Kerry said and motioned for Rick to sit down at the table. We men will sit here and discuss the matters at hand.

Aileen flipped Kerry off then and the two of them shared hateful glances until breaking down and laughing. We'll be back, she said, guiding Mary Ann out the back door.

Listen, Kerry said to Rick when the door closed, his voice lowering to a conspiratorial whisper, I've dated some of those women in my day. I've seen more than my share of vindictive bitches.

I hear you, Rick said.

I mean it, Kerry said and drained what was left of his whiskey and filled it back up. I dated this one girl and she called the cops on me. I didn't do anything at all, Rick. Swear on the Virgin Mother. She called and told 'em I'd laid my hands on her. They showed up, took one look at her, and then they apologized to me. To me, he said and slapped the table again.

That's trouble right there, Rick said.

You bet it is, Kerry said. Course, Aileen never understood that. She was always saying to me, Well, what did you do? She could never get that I was just minding my business and this whole thing was thrust upon me. Hell, she's probably out there right now with Mary Ann talking about how I was some kind of monster before we got together.

Rick turned the glass around on the table and lifted it up. He looked at the ring of sweat it left and then touched it with his finger.

I go off at the mouth sometimes, Kerry said. Tell me, he said, what happened with this Audrey bitch?

I don't know, Rick said.

C'mon, Kerry said. You're talking to your buddy for life here.

Mary Ann and me, he said, we agreed we weren't going to get into this. That was our deal before we

100

moved here.

Get into what? Kerry said.

This whole thing, Rick said. I mean, it was a shit-storm, Kerry. Worst period of my life. No doubt about it. If someone asked me to write down the worst times of my life and put them in order this would be at number one. Number two? That'd be a ways down the list.

I'm going to be honest with you, Kerry said. And I haven't told anybody this. You really are my best friend though, that much is true. Before you and Mary Ann came along, before you moved here last summer, I wouldn't of even considered telling anybody this.

What? Rick said.

I just want to impart that on you, Kerry said. I just want you to let that soak for a while. Not another person on the face of this here Earth would I tell this to. I'm not trying to get sentimental, he said and then wiped his hands on the thighs of his jeans. I'm not trying to get over-emotional on you, buddy. But I think friendship's an important thing. Maybe the most important.

I'd have to agree, Rick said.

You bet, Kerry said. About that night, with the gal who called the cops.

Friendship's important, Rick said. I agree about that.

Sure you would, Kerry said.

What do you think they're talking about out there? Rick said and nodded at the back door.

Who knows? Kerry said. Who knows what women talk about? But listen, he said.

There was this girl, Rick said.

There's always a girl, Kerry said.

She was a freshman girl, Rick said.

A freshman girl? Kerry said.

Kerry, she was fifteen but it was like I'd known her my whole life.

Who was? This freshman girl?

That's right, Rick said. And there was something so familiar about her. She came into my class and nobody wanted anything to do with the girl. The other kids shunned her like she had the plague or something. You have to have somebody, you know? Just somebody for those times you can't figure things out on your own. That's my philosophy on the matter.

Wait, where was this? Kerry said.

At the high school, Rick said. The high school I worked at.

Okay, Kerry said. Just getting this straight.

And she needed a friend, Rick said.

Hold on, Kerry said. I think maybe the girls are coming back.

I'm trying to tell you, Rick said. It was Audrey's fault. That's all. Mary Ann and me were doing really well. We were getting along so good and then that Audrey bitch stuck her nose in my business.

Audrey, Kerry said.

Audrey, Rick said.

Kerry reached for his glass of whiskey and tipped it over. A few drops of liquor and a splattering of melted ice seeped out onto the table. Damn it, he said and rushed to the sink to get a towel. I need to clean this up.

I agree with you, Rick said. Friendship's important,

right?

You got it, Kerry said and pressed the towel down on the spill. The most important thing, if you ask me.

That's what I think too, Rick said, never lifting his eyes. That's why I'm just glad we're all friends. I can't tell you how grateful I am about that. That's just about the best thing to happen to us in forever.

As he was saying that the back door opened and Aileen came in. Her look had hardened. She looked at the spill on the table and then at Kerry.

I spilled my drink, Kerry said to her. I'm sorry. Honey, I'm sorry.

Not far behind Aileen was Mary Ann. Her face was flush red and the men could see where she'd been crying. She took a deep breath and when she went to exhale what exited her mouth was a sick-sounding sob.

Fifteen years old, Aileen said without emotion.

Friendship, Rick said, still looking at the ring of sweat under his glass.

Fifteen years old, Aileen said again.

It's probably the most important thing there is, Rick said and waited for someone to agree.

BEHOLD,
✪ I COME AS A THIEF ✪

THEY WERE TIRED from all of the sex. It was the
weekend, which meant it was time for having sex and
walking around their apartment without any clothes on.
Every weekend worked that way. They would get home
from work, take off their clothes, and have sex until
they got tired. Then they would walk around the
apartment and eat and drink and watch TV without
their clothes on until they were ready to have sex
again.

There's something on the TV, he said to her.
Something about an earthquake.

She stood in front of a window beside the TV. She
didn't have any clothes on. She patted her flat stomach
with her hands and looked down at the gas station next
door. People parked at the pumps and walked in and
out of the building. What's that? she said.

There was an earthquake in Japan, he said.

On the TV was a news program about the earthquake in Japan. There were several pictures of Japanese people standing in the streets, crying and looking shell-shocked. Sometimes the pictures of Japanese people looking upset and confused were replaced by pictures of rubble and ambulances and people digging through what was left of their homes.

I'm hungry, she said, still patting her stomach by the window. I'm always so hungry after having sex.

He was too. Every weekend, when they had sex and walked around the apartment without any clothes on, he was starving the whole time. It took a lot out of him having sex like that. They were very adventurous and tried many positions. Sometimes, between positions, he would lean down and ask her if she liked a new position and she, being quite a positive and supportive person, would always say yes, she liked the new position.

We have leftovers in the fridge, he said to her, trying to help with the problem of hunger.

I never feel like leftovers, she said, watching a couple exit a pick-up truck and walk hand-in-hand to the gas station. They had on matching sweatshirts and their hair was cut similarly. I always look at the tupperware, she said, and think to myself, enough is enough.

He didn't say anything. He never felt that way, not really. And besides, he was too busy looking at her nice body and thinking that maybe he'd like to have sex with her in a little bit, after they'd eaten and rested and watched some TV, of course.

People here are stunned, the TV said. Their entire world has been shaken.

Tell you what, he said to her. I'll see what I can do.

The two of them went into the kitchen and he opened up the fridge. There were stacks of leftovers on the shelves and he removed them and put them on the counter by the stove. There was rice and bacon and some pork chops they hadn't cared for all that much. He got out a skillet from the cabinets and filled it with oil.

Here's an old trick, he said to her. I call this one Bachelor's Surprise.

As he turned on the heat she sat down at their kitchen table and crossed her legs. It felt good to be naked all weekend. It was something she looked forward to. She'd been spending her weekends naked for so long she barely remembered a time before doing so. Whenever she put on clothes to go to the store or to run an errand or to go back to work on Monday she felt odd and out of place. She liked being naked and she liked sitting there in the kitchen and watching him cook while naked.

Let's fry that rice, he said, dumping the rice into the skillet. He got a wooden spoon from a drawer and pushed the rice around some. Hey, he said to her. What're you thinking about?

Being naked, she said and uncrossed and crossed her legs. I'm thinking about how much I like being naked and I'm thinking about the earthquake.

What about the earthquake? he said.

I don't know, she said. Earthquakes are scary. One minute you're standing there, eating or drinking or whatever, and the next you're not. The ground opens up and you're gone.

It's awful, he said, turning over the tupperware that

106

held the bacon and scraping it into the skillet with the rice. You can try your hardest, he said, but you can't predict something like that happening.

You can't, she said. She watched him cook and watched how his naked body moved as he stirred the skillet. I mean, she said, there could be an earthquake right now and we'd be in a whole lot of trouble. We could be the ones on the news.

We could, he said. He got the tupperware with the pork chops and he cut them into little bites and plopped them into the skillet with the rice and the bacon. He got a bottle of soy sauce out of the cabinet too and he poured some into the skillet and swished it around. Hey, he said. This is going to be pretty good.

I'm thinking about this earthquake I was in once, she said.

You were in an earthquake? he said.

I've been in a couple, she said. She looked down at her breasts and, for no reason at all, ran a finger over one of them. The breast moved and then stopped. One when I was little, she said. It wasn't very big.

How old? he said. He was still frying the food in the skillet.

Maybe eight, she said. All the cups and plates rattled around a bit.

That's not too bad, he said, thinking about the Japanese people on the TV.

No, she said.

What about the other one? he said.

What other one? she said. She didn't know what he was talking about.

The other earthquake, he said. He poured some

more soy sauce into the skillet with the rice and the bacon and the pieces of pork chop. You said you'd been through a couple.

Oh, she said and remembered then. That was just a few years ago. When I lived out west.

Out west, he repeated. That was before they knew one another, before they spent their weekends having sex and walking around naked. Remembering that made him remember having sex and suddenly he wanted to have sex very badly.

Out west, she repeated. That was when I was living with Horace in that old house. You remember that old house.

He did remember that old house. He'd gone there to pick her and her things up after they'd fallen in love over the telephone. He pulled up in front in his friend's truck and loaded all of her things off the old house's porch and took her away. He hadn't met Horace but he'd heard him yelling and screaming in the background of their phone calls. He also saw Horace standing in the window upstairs. He was crying, confused. I remember that old house, he said to her.

It wasn't built too good, she said. It was an old and when that earthquake hit it swayed back and forth like it was going to fall right over.

It was an old house, he said.

The Bachelor's Surprise was almost done at that point so he turned down the heat. Food's almost done, he said to her.

Me and Horace were in bed, she said to him. We were always in bed back then. It was the weekend and that's what we did.

He got plates out from the cabinet and set them on the counter next to the stove and the skillet full of Bachelor's Surprise.

And that old house, she said, was swaying back and forth and it woke us up. I woke up and I said, Horace, I think we're having an earthquake. And he jumped up, scared as hell, and screamed, Damn it, we got to get outside, and ran out the door.

He spooned out some of the Bachelor's Surprise onto the plates and pictured Horace screaming and running out the door. Food's up, he said.

He was naked, she said. We were always naked back then, that's what we did on the weekends, and he ran outside and was screaming some more and running around.

Food's ready, he said.

She got a plate of Bachelor's Surprise and she took a fork he handed her and scooped up a bite and chewed it. She told him it was good and continued with her story.

And here's the best part of it, she said. There'd just been an earthquake, right? So all the neighbors are coming out of their houses and looking around to see what was what. And there was Horace, naked as the day he was born, standing by the grill and screaming and screaming.

He took a bite of the Bachelor's Surprise and swallowed it down. He took another bite.

Oh, she said between bites, that was the best. We were both spooked as could be at that point. We stayed up the rest of the night, drinking and worrying there was going to be another earthquake. What's that called?

she said.

What's what called? he said. He was finished with his Bachelor's Surprise.

The ones that come afterward, she said. They're earthquakes too, but never as big as the original ones.

Aftershocks, he said, scraping his Bachelor's Surprise down the drain and thinking about getting a drink from the fridge. He was thinking about getting a drink and then maybe putting some clothes on. He wanted to go for a walk. He felt like maybe the house was swaying a bit and it made him uncomfortable and it made him forget about wanting to have sex.

Aftershocks, she said. She was almost done with her Bachelor's Surprise and she uncrossed and crossed her legs again. I read that somewhere, she said, thinking about maybe wanting to have sex again.

MONSIEUR
✪ AND MADEMOISELLE ✪

ANGRY AND HUNGOVER, she says We've got to stop this.

She's in the living room floor scrubbing a stain. Behind her a trail of glass and half a dozen overturned books. This is her natural way of spending a Saturday afternoon, how she goes about once we finally drag ourselves out of bed. I'm tending to the bottle of Tylenol in the bathroom and gulping down handful after handful of water and hoping the thudding will slow down.

You always make a big deal out of it, I say between gulps. Everyone had a good time.

Nobody had a good time, she says. I don't know if you've noticed, she says, but less and less people come every time we throw one of these things. Word's getting around just how screwed up we are.

I give myself a good healthy stretch and then

scratch all the right places. In the living room I watch her work that stain from the doorway. I can't remember if it's wine or blood or both. I'm gonna make some breakfast, I tell her. You want some breakfast?

Terry, she says to me. God damn it. That's always your answer. I'll make some breakfast. Sometimes breakfast doesn't cut it.

The kitchen itself is lined with empty bottles and the sink full of dishes. I open the fridge and look inside. Most everything is gone. We throw the kind of shindigs where people help themselves. They eat chunks of cheese, grapes, hell, the butter if they're feeling up to it. There's not much left except a pound of sausage and a roll of instant biscuits. I grab those and the bag of flour out of the cabinet next to the fridge. Then the phone rings.

Hello, I hear her say when she answers. She's silent for a second and then starts in with the apologies. Oh god, she says, I'm so sorry. We're so sorry Pam. I mean it, we're sorry. You know how it gets. People start drinking and things happen.

She's apologizing to Pam, her friend from the book club. Pam always comes to these things and always ends up offended. She's got real sensitive sensibilities. Her husband's no better. Last night I was giving him some shit about being from Oklahoma and he got so wound up he stormed off.

No, I hear her say, Terry didn't mean anything by it. He forgets what's polite conversation. No, she says. No, I don't think so. No.

I get the sausage frying in a pan on the stove and look out the window over the sink. Our deck is always the worst. People go out there and smoke and leave their butts and drinks. Sometimes they break the chairs or the rails. That's usually where I like to go when it gets too stuffy or need a moment to myself. Last night there was a fine thing out there smoking these long, thin cigarettes by the woodpile. She came with this guy I know from work. We all call him Tiny. I'll let you figure it out. Anyway, she came in with him and hung up their coats. Then she offers me her hand, the way women used to do, and waits for me to give it a kiss. She called me monsieur. Pleasure to make your acquaintance, monsieur, she said.

Mademoiselle, I said back to her.

Well, she says coming into the kitchen with the sponge she'd been using on the carpet, that was Pam. She said I'm not invited to the book club anymore. Are you happy now?

Am I happy? I say, looking out at the back porch, at a spot just over the rail. There's a paper plate barely hanging on. It must've rained this morning because it's turned soggy and frowns at the edges. Right there is where that woman was smoking her cigarettes. No, I say, I can't say I'm happy.

Well, she says, you shouldn't be. This is getting to the point of no return, you know. It's getting to a place where something's got to give.

In the frying pan on the stove the sausage is browned and I reach for the flour and get a nice and thick gravy going. Then I remember the biscuits and line them up in dots in the pan and set the oven up. Pam's boring, I say. And her husband's no better.

Terry, she says.

They can both go to fucking Oklahoma for all I care, I say.

You know, she says, fixing breakfast isn't going to solve everything. You always think it will, but it won't.

You want to put the coffee on? I say to her.

Are you listening to me? she says. I can't be married to somebody who turns into a monster.

All right, I say, I'll get the coffee going.

She storms off to the living room and stands there and huffs. That's what she does. She's like a child sometimes in how she gets her anger out. I kid you not, you get her upset enough and she'll pound the table like an upset toddler. It's a sight to see.

The coffee's going now and the sausage and gravy are warming and the biscuits are in and I'm standing here feeling about a thousand times better. I've go to the point where I can shake a hangover in less than an hour. All I've got to the do is drink a shit-ton of water and focus on things. Right now it's that spot out there. I walked out last night and that woman was smoking her cigarette and I said to her, smooth as I could manage, Well, hello there mademoiselle.

She turned and gave me a smile. I'd said the secret word, I think. I picked up on her code. Why monsieur, she said, fancy meeting you in a place like this.

That was that. What happened next was sealed from that point on. Looking at that spot, next to the woodpile, I can only imagine there's probably a place where the grass has been pushed down. An imprint of her. Probably half of that cigarette she was smoking. I remind myself to go out there later and see if I can find it. It's something I wouldn't mind keeping around.

114

I'm sorry, she says, collapsing in a chair at the kitchen table. My head won't stop pounding and I couldn't feel worse. Didn't mean to make a big deal out of it, she says.

It's all right, I say.

The food's pretty much done. The biscuits are a little undercooked, on the doughy side, but that's how she likes them. I get a plate loaded up, split them long-wise, and ladle on the sausage and gravy. There's steam rising up and when I set it in front of her with a cup of coffee she's smiling.

Eat up, I say. It'll help.

It will, she says. It always does.

I get myself a plate and grab some pepper. I'd prefer the whole thing spicier, stronger, but she doesn't care for the heat. Sometimes you have to do things for other people. Once I've got it covered I grab my mug from the dishwasher and have a seat. She's already digging in, forking big wads of biscuit into her mouth and swallowing happily.

Maybe later, she says, we can go to the movies.

Yeah, I say, still thinking about the woodpile. That'd be nice.

It would, she says. We haven't been in a long time.

No ma'am, I say.

Maybe we can get gussied up, she says. Put on some nice clothes and grab some dinner and then go catch a movie.

I'd like that, I say.

Would you? she says.

I would, I say.

She gives me a look then like all is forgiven. Her

plate is half-empty and I can tell the hangover's starting to lift. She doesn't care about Pam anymore. About that damned book club. And she sure as shit doesn't care about the carpet in the living room or anything else. Everything that has passed has passed and we're squared right away. She even stretches her leg under the table and traces my knee with the point of her foot. This is her signal she likes to give sometimes. It says, Let's finish this up and start something else. I take a sip of my coffee and nod, let her know I've picked up her code.

Everything's solved, everything's perfect, and then the phone rings again.

IF I CAN JUST
✪ PUT INTO WORDS ✪

SHE CAME HOME from work and saw him sitting and smoking a cigarette in his chair on the balcony. He was watching the trees in the backyard. Hey Stu, she yelled at him from the driveway. Hey Stu, what're you looking at?

His answer was mumbled. She chose not to ask again and carried her things inside the house. It was a nice house, nicer than they could afford, particularly now that Stu hadn't drawn a check in three months. The floors were all hardwood, the molding custom-made, the rooms intricate in their angles and design. Every room was clean––that was Clarissa's doing–– except for Stu's office, which was the room right off the living area. He had his big desk in there and the top of it was covered in scraps of paper and manuscript pages with big jags of pen marks ripping across them.

She climbed the stairs and found the bed still unmade. There were a few beer bottles on the nightstand. Through the French doors she could see Stu sitting there on the balcony.

Hey honey, she said, opening the doors and stepping out. I asked what you were doing.

Stu began to turn to answer her, but paused like there was something he couldn't take his eyes off of. He said, How was your day?

Fine, she said and settled in the chair next to his and looked at all the bottles and spent butts at his feet. He was in his pajamas still. What're you watching out here?

There he goes, Stu said and pointed at a cluster of trees near the back of the yard. Look right there.

Clarissa looked but she couldn't make anything out. What am I looking for here?

That's Butler, Stu said.

Butler?

Butler, Stu said and pointed once more, this time his finger shaking with impatience.

Clarissa tried again and this time she saw a gray squirrel hustling down the trunk of a tree. Is Butler a squirrel? she said.

You bet your ass, Stu said and scooped up a pad of paper from the ground. He held it in his lap and scribbled furiously with a pen. He's been at it all day, he said.

At what? she said.

See, Stu said, pausing writing long enough to answer, there's a couple of ladies in the trees. Philly and Bernice. Few hours ago he was chasing Philly around that there tree and Bernice was chasing the both of them. At one point, he stopped, reversed, and then got to chasing Bernice while Philly chased them.

Stu, Clarissa said, we are talking about squirrels here, right?

He tapped the pad of paper with his pen until he looked up and gave her a sharp stare. Goddamn it, he said, that's no way to talk about my work.

Clarissa leaned over and looked at the paper. Every inch of it was covered in scratches and doodles describing and depicting the actions of squirrels. There were hastily written notes and whole diagrams of how Butler and Philly and Bernice had chased each other. She gave up and leaned back in her chair and closed her eyes. She thought of the bills sitting on the kitchen counter downstairs. She pictured the ledger in her checkbook and the number that was always shrinking.

If I can get this down, Stu said, if I can do this justice, we're looking at a bestseller here. If I can just put into words what's happening out here on a daily basis we won't have anything to worry about anymore.

That's a tall order, Clarissa said, eyes still closed.

You bet it is, Stu said. Then, surprised, he said, Oh jesus, Philly just climbed out onto that high limb. Oh jesus, I don't like the looks of this.

Clarissa saw Philly in her mind, a squirrel with wire-like hair scooting carefully out onto the farthest part of a limb before looking down and venturing farther.

Stu said, I don't think she can take it anymore. Philly, he yelled, Philly.

There was a rustle of leaves. The wooden crack of

the limb shifting.

My god, he yelled. She's spiraling down, she's moving so goddamn fast. My god, Philly, he said.

Clarissa couldn't help but smile. He'd done it. He'd really done it.

✪ KNIGHTS ✪

I GOT WASPS, my cousin said.

Wasps? I said. Tully, what do you mean you have wasps?

I mean I got more wasps than you ever saw. Flying around. Crawling on the screens. You look anywhere in this here house and you can bet your ass you're gonna see a wasp.

Sounds awful, I said. Call an exterminator.

An exterminator? He laughed good and hard. You call a goddamn exterminator. I got a rolled-up Sports Illustrated and it's doing the job just fine.

I pinched the bridge of my nose and closed my eyes. My cousin Tully was a real pain in the pass. Always had been. Even growing up, he was too much to handle. As I got older I'd learned to keep my distance so I didn't have to deal with it anymore.

Call an exterminator or don't, I said. Quite frankly, I don't give a shit. I was just calling to check in and see what the hell happened with Sarah Joe.

Sarah Joe, he said, his voice sounding like he was remembering somebody he hadn't thought of in years. That right there is a complicated subject.

Sure, I said and began the process of getting off the phone. But anyway, I said, give me a ring if you need anything.

Tell you what, Tully said, swing by here tomorrow. I'll fix us up some cocktails and you can see can an eyeful of this wasp situation.

More often than not I would've just said I had something to do, it's how I'd been handling Tully for years, but both of us would've known that was a lie. The city had laid me and another dozen fellas off for the winter and my days were free as free could be. So I went over there the next afternoon, over to Tully's house behind the Dollar Store.

The second I walked up on his porch I saw the problem. Up in the corner was a nest the size of a desk globe. It was grayish and looked like somebody had fashioned it out of paper mâché.

Tully opened the door while I was standing there staring at it. Looks like you already found the mothership, he said.

Inside it didn't take long to see what was going on. There was a wasp tiptoeing across the nearest window. Another on the wall.

Goddamn, I said. Tully, you got to do something about this.

He grinned a little and picked his rolled-up Sports Illustrated off his coffee table. This is step one, he said and swatted the wasp on the window. It hit square and the wasp fell to the floor, where there was already eight or nine others piled up. The window was covered in streaks from where he'd splattered them earlier. Step two, he said, is the strongest gin and tonic you ever had.

He got to work making it in the kitchen, stopping only to swat a pair of wasps by the stove, and I took a seat at the table. It was my grandparents' old one that Tully got after Grandma passed. I'd sat there for hours upon hours playing Five Hundred and trying to get Grandpa to talk baseball or the war.

Here's what I figure, Tully said, stirring my drink with his finger, we got on our hands right now the warmest snap December ever saw. Seventy, eighty degrees. These here buggers, they're confused. They're sluggish. They get in here and it's almost like they're looking to get put out of their misery.

I swear, I said, I never saw anything like this weather.

No sir, Tully said and handed me my drink. You didn't get winters like this when we were young 'uns.

I sucked some down and it was more gin than tonic. A sting of the alcohol shot through me in a hurry. It's good, I said.

Tully sat down in the seat my grandma always sat at, the seat that used to be closest to the phone and the sugar bowl. They don't mean harm, he said. I've been stung once so far and that was my fault. I sat down on the couch without looking. Other than that, they ain't the worst roommates I've ever had.

Just as soon as he'd finished saying that he got a look in his eye, like a predator catching sight of some prey. He lifted out of the chair with the magazine in hand and stalked across the kitchen and back into the living room. There was a wasp in the corner and he snuck up and smacked it a good one. I guess that didn't do it though because he had to smack it a few more times on the floor.

That's when I noticed the trash bags. There were three of them leaning against the wall, two of them tied shut and the third stuffed too full to close. Peeking out of the top was a light purple fabric. The sleeve of a woman's blouse.

That Sarah Joe's stuff? I asked him.

Tully was coming back to the table, but he stopped and looked over at the bags. He flipped them off halfheartedly and gave me a smile. Yeah, he said. She left some shit here. Some tops, some jeans. Most of it's stuff she doesn't really wear anymore, but I figure she'll be back one way or another here 'fore too long.

I waited for him to sit down and have a drink. So, I said, what the hell happened there?

Oh hell, he said. I don't know. Who the fuck knows with a woman?

Aunt Sissy was the one who'd told me. I'd ran into her at the store and she'd talked my ear off for the better part of a half hour. She wouldn't stop going on about how worthless Sarah Joe was and how worthless she'd always been.

I told him, she'd said to me, there in the bread aisle, all the people trying to get around us. God help me, I told him. I said, Tully, baby, you go looking for love under a rock and you're bound to find a slug.

It seemed that Sarah Joe had reunited with her old flame after he'd finally gotten out of jail. He'd been in three years for meth and somehow they'd carried on via letters the whole time.

Here's what I figured out, Tully said between drinks. She had a P.O. box down at the post-office. I can't even begin to tell you how she managed the secrecy. Where'd she find the time to write those letters? You tell me 'cause I don't know. And get this, this here's the icing on the cake: I talked to her momma the other day and she said Sarah Joe's been running up to Baldwin every now and then to visit the fucker. I asked her why she didn't tell me and she said everyone thought I knew already. Now, what'd you think of that?

I shook my head.

Exactly, Tully said. Exactly.

He was about to go on, but a wasp dive-bombed us and then sped off to a light on the ceiling. We watched it for a second and then it just did the same thing again.

That's what I can't stand, Tully said, gripping his magazine. I'd be fine with these sons of bitches if they didn't get wild every now and then. We'd be just peachy-fucking-keen if I didn't have these rogues getting a wild hair every now and then and buzzing my face.

Tully got up and tracked the wasp. It dived him again and he took a swing at it. Then it flew off into the living room and all the fight seemed to drain out of Tully. His shoulders sagged and his bottom lip stuck out like a boy who just got whupped.

When he sat back down I was about to ask him more about Sarah Joe, but didn't have the heart. He looked about as beat as a man could look. Besides, Aunt Sissy had already told me everything there was to tell. How Sarah Joe had emptied their checking account the day her ex got free and how nobody, not even her momma, had seen or heard from her since.

I could tell Tully was looking past me and staring at those bags in the other room. He was turning his gin and tonic around and wiping the sweat off the glass. It seemed like he was just a second or two from losing it when a smile broke on his face and he looked at me and said, You know what I've been thinking about lately?

What's that? I said.

You remember, he said, when we used to play out by Grandpa's woodpile?

Sure, I said. I remembered it clear as day. Out there by grandpa's shed he'd kept a pile, maybe ten feet long and five feet high, a bright blue tarp fastened on. I said, We used to play that game. Knights.

That's right, Tully said. He had a drink and grinned. I don't know why, he said, but I've been thinking we called it Castle or something like that. But you're right. Knights. We'd both get us a stick or something, he said, holding up his magazine like it was a sword.

And we'd both take turns, I said, remembering. One of us would be the lookout and the other one the defender.

Right, he said. That's what got me thinking, these here wasps. 'Cause most of the time we'd pretend monsters and the like were attacking the pile, but then sometimes some bugs or spiders or beer would come out and I'd say, Make ready your weapons. Like we were in a movie.

I laughed just thinking about it. Back then Tully was just this runt of a kid, the boy everyone picked on, but when we'd play and he'd give the command his voice would turn strong and impressive.

Shit fire, I said, we'd be out there just wailing on that woodpile with these sticks and ball bats and old golf clubs and Grandpa would lean out the door and give us hell.

Boys, Tully said, doing his best impression, if you don't settle down I'm gonna whip your asses red.

The impression was so good I couldn't help but laugh. But that didn't last long. It happened quick, the change in mood. I don't know if Tully got to thinking about Grandpa right then, but I sure did. About how he'd just wasted away, there on a foldout couch in their living room, not ten feet from the very table we were sitting around.

Jesus, I said, trying to keep it together, I ought to get out of here, Tully.

You sure? he said. I got a half bottle of Seagram's in the freezer with your name on it.

Yeah, I said. It's getting late. You know how it goes.

Tully nodded. Reckon I do, he said.

On my way out I saw a few more wasps hanging around. One was on a side-table, acting like he was thinking about climbing up the side of a lamp. Another, this one sluggish like Tully was talking about, crawling in circles on the floor.

Well shit, Tully said, looking down at it with a face full of pity.

Take care of yourself, I said. I mean it, I said, give me a ring if you need anything.

You bet, Tully said, still looking down.

What I wanted was to make a joke, to lighten the mood I guess, so I yelled out, in that same dramatic voice Tully always used to use. I yelled, Make ready your weapons.

But if Tully heard me he didn't act like it. He seemed more concerned with that wasp struggling at his feet. Seemed like he was trying to work up the nerve to smash it, but just couldn't make himself do it.

✪ LIVE OFF THE LAND ✪

IT WAS TWO-THIRTY and all the food and booze was gone and drunk and the two couples settled into the living room. As they did Harris turned on the TV with the remote. A basketball game filled the screen. A team in green jerseys was playing a team in yellow in a nearly empty arena.

My god, Bessie said, I thought it was later than that.

Later than what? Harris said. He was sitting in his recliner next to the couch where Bessie was cramped in with their friends Steve and Alice. Harris had the remote in his hand, extended like he would be changing the channel at any moment.

I mean, Bessie said drunkenly, later than a basketball game would be on.

That's in Alaska, Steve said, leaning forward and squinting. It's earlier there. Still late, but earlier.

Bessie seemed confused. She turned and looked across Steve to Alice. She wanted to see if she was confused too. Earlier? she said. You're drunk, doll.

Everyone's drunk, Harris said.

Speak for yourself, Alice chimed in. I'm not drunk. If we're going to be honest, I didn't get enough to drink. You yahoos drank up most of the booze trading shots.

Honey, Steve said, you're drunk.

Don't bet on it, she said and crossed her legs.

That's the nature of the beast, Bessie said and then stopped.

Harris waited for her to finish. She had a habit, when drunk, of starting to say something and then letting it drift off like a balloon. Experience had taught him it would've been better to just let it go and watch the game, but he couldn't. He said, What is?

What is what?

What's the nature of the beast?

Oh, Bessie said. I'm just saying that's what happens when you get a couple of men together and the booze comes out.

What does that mean? Steve said.

Wait, Alice said, what time is it in Alaska?

Ten or eleven, Harris said and set down the remote.

Bessie laughed. Harris thinks he knows everything about Alaska. Just ask him. He's a real expert on the subject.

Now hold on, Harris said. I'd like to hear what she has to say. What happens when you get men together, Bessie?

You know what I mean, she said. You get some booze out and you puff up your chests and start taking shots to prove who the biggest, baddest man is.

That's right, Alice said. You just hit that right on the head. You just landed on the problem. The men start competing and don't leave hardly any behind. Not enough for anybody to get good and drunk on anyway.

Steve said, Alice, you're plenty drunk. Just listen to yourself.

Alice got off the couch and walked a shaky line up and down the floor. When she finished she touched her nose with her finger and took a bow. Sober as a nun on Sunday, she said.

I tell you what, Harris said, you want some booze we'll go get you some booze. No problem. Unless you just want a reason to sit there and complain.

That's my Harris, Bessie said, a knight in shining armor.

Unamused, Harris stared back at her. Do ya'll want something else to drink or not?

Hey, Steve said, I doubt anything's open. And besides, I'm in no shape to drive.

Now who's drunk? Alice said.

Ted's might be open still, Harris said. And I'm fine to drive. No problems.

Here comes Harris on his white steep, Bessie said.

Steed, Harris said.

What did I say? she asked her friends.

It's fine, Steve said.

Well, Bessie said, whatever. All I'm saying is that Harris always wants to be the hero. He always wants to be the savior.

Bessie, he said.

What?

They looked at each other, Harris' face unchanging and Bessie staring back until her gaze fell to the floor.

Steve broke the silence. Let me grab my boots, he

said.

What do you want to drink? Harris asked Alice.

I don't care the least bit, she said.

Nah, Harris said. You name it and we'll get it. Rum? Vodka? Shit, we'll pick out some champagne if that's what tickles your fancy.

Truth be told, she said, I don't think this is so hot of an idea. Let's call it a night. Let's just pack it in.

Nonsense, Harris said. Steve, toss me my keys.

With them in hand the two men went outside. It was chilly, cold for that early in September, and the streets were empty save for a few scattered leaves. Harris pressed a button on his key ring and the garage door growled to life and started to lift. As they waited Harris took a deep breath and watched his exhale turn to steam.

Colder than a tit out here, he said.

You bet, Steve answered.

Stepping through a crowd of tools and shovels and rakes, they got into the Ford Harris and Bessie shared and he pulled out and maneuvered around Steve's station wagon and into the road. Harris paused there as he put the car in drive.

Ted's is this way? he said, unsure. Right?

Sure thing, Steve said. Say, he said, you really think this is a good idea?

It's the only idea, Harris said and pressed the gas. We'll never hear the end of it if we don't go.

I guess that's right, Steve said.

I know it, Harris said. There's something in Bessie where she can't let anything go. I tell you, she won't let a single thing go. Ever. She's like one of those, uh, what do you call those damn things? Those plants?

Plants?

You know, he said, his fingers made into teeth and put up to his mouth, the one that eats things.

I got to say, Steve said, I don't think I know what the hell you're talking about.

Harris' face scrunched up like he was trying to wrench out the information. As it did the car drifted into a neighboring lane. Harris paid no attention until it reached the shoulder and the rumble strip shook them.

Damn it, he said and corrected the wheel. What the hell are those things called? I can see 'em like they were right here in front of me.

Sorry, Steve said. I'm not much on plants.

Me neither, Harris said. Not much on plants at all.

Ted's Spirits was in a strip mall eight blocks away. On one end of the shopping center was a twenty-four hour Kroger's and on the other a Radio Shack. Ted's was in the middle and it was immediately clear it was closed for the night. The light were switched off and the windows gated shut.

Well, son of a bitch, Harris shouted and punched his dashboard.

Thought that was a possibility, Steve said.

That's a shame, Harris said. Never understood for the life of me why liquor stores weren't open all night. Situation like this happens more than you like to think.

Too many unsavory characters, Steve said.

Shit, Harris said. It's the same case every time. Too many folks incapable of handling their own business and ruining it for the rest of us.

Yes sir, Steve said.

Tell you what, Harris said and nudged Steve, pick you out a rock and let's bust in there. We'll clean the place out and be gone before anyone's the wiser.

Steve looked at his friend. He couldn't tell if he was being serious. Yeah, he said. Right.

Yeah, yeah, Harris said. I could do it though, if I wanted. You don't know this about me, he said, but I'm a man of means. If I wanted, if the idea struck me, I could go in there and take anything I wanted. No problem at all.

Sure you could, Steve said. But if you don't mind, Jessie James, let's just head on over to the Kroger's and see what there is to see.

When he quit talking Steve flashed a smile at Harris and expected one in return. He was disappointed though as he could tell Harris didn't like his joke one bit.

I swear to god, he said as he put the car in drive, ain't nobody listens to one goddamn word I say anymore. He drove across the parking lot and into the closest spot to the store. As he opened his door he was saying, Everyone nowadays thinks they are experts on everything.

The automatic doors whooshed open and let them in. The store was blindingly bright, cold and empty save for a single open register and the sound of someone running a buffer somewhere. Harris ambled in the direction of the liquor aisle, Steve close behind.

I was telling Bessie a while back, he said, that I got half a notion to pack it all up and head for greener pastures. Say sayonara to all this bullshit and go and live off the land somewhere.

Live off the land, Steve repeated.

You got it, Harris said. They'd arrived at the liquor aisle where there cases upon cases of beer stacked on the shelves, color-coded and sorted by brand. Harris grabbed some Miller Lites and said, I'd like to get away from this shit we call a life. I'm sick of having it easy. I want to get my hands dirty, work up some calluses, you know. Go to sleep at night, exhausted and proud.

Steve grabbed a beer for himself and said, Sounds good.

I figure it wouldn't take much, Harris said, leading Harris over to the shelf with the wine. Near the bottom was a row of cheap champagnes, the bottles green and topped with golden foil. All I'd need, he said, grabbing one at random, is a few acres, my axe, and some good ol' fashion know-how.

I reckon that's about all it takes, Steve said.

The only register with its light on was Number 8. Underneath, looking just about as bored as anybody the two men had ever seen, was a thirty-something cashier. She was on the frumpy side, but her face was nice enough and her hair was done up in a red handkerchief with a lot of charm.

When Harris placed the alcohol on the belt she whistled and said, Looks like somebody's having a party.

You got it, Harris said. Don't stop 'til the sun comes up.

The cashier smiled at him and then at Steve. He returned it and then looked away. He stared off across the store, into space, and then finally focused on an end-cap twenty yards away. It was advertising a new cartoon movie for kids and there were monsters of all different colors and shapes and sizes on the cardboard cutout. With no idea why, they reminded him of the plant Harris had been talking about in the car.

Steve remembered sitting in his seventh grade biology class and sitting in a dark room and watching a movie on a projector. It was a film about flora––he remembered that word––and all the different kinds of plants in the world. The shaky picture played on a white pull-down screen and he could see the plant on there, its triangle-shaped teeth wide open, like regular everyday leaves, until a fly landed and the trap sprung on it.

What was the name of it? he thought. It was right there.

Hey, Harris said, you up for it?

What's that? he said.

Me and Kelly here, Harris said, holding up the champagne and gesturing at the cashier, we're gonna head up to Alaska and live off the land. You in?

Steve looked from Harris to the cashier. He was half-serious while Kelly the cashier was only playing along. We should probably check with our wives first, Steve said.

Harris' face soured. There you go, he said, pissing all over our parade.

He didn't speak to Harris until they got back to the car. As he tossed the beer and champagne into the backseat he said, You're not gonna believe this, but Bessie has ruined every goddamn dream I ever had. Every last one.

Where would you go? Steve said.

Huh?

If you were gonna live off the land?

It's like I told her, he said, Alaska's an option. Parts of it anyway. Canada too. Saskatchewan. Hell, maybe ever Siberia. I told her, same as I'm telling you right now, I'm dead-serious about this.

I know you are, Steve said. What'd she say?

What'd she say? Harris said. She said I was crazy. Steve, I'm not making this up at all. She laughed right in my face.

They drove back to the house, past a cop waiting in a roadside lot, in silence the whole way. Harris kept steady at the wheel, his face twisting as if he were in a constant conversation in his head, while Steve kept trying to remember the name of that plant. He could see it, that grainy killer, but just couldn't catch the word.

At the house they pulled back into the garage and stumbled past the tools and junk again on their way inside. To their surprise, Bessie and Alice were three-quarters of the way into a bottle of Southern Comfort.

Looky here, Bessie said, shaking the bottle. We found a secret stash.

Harris stood in the door, holding the booze he'd bought. He looked pale to Steve, about ready to fall over or storm through the house. Where'd you get that? he said.

In the basement, Alice said, her words slurring. We went explooooooring.

She had drawn the last word out and when she finished both of the women burst into fits of hysterical laughter.

Why's that so funny? Harris asked them.

It's nothing, Bessie said. Anyway, it was in one of the boxes we never unpacked from the move.

No, Harris said, dropping the case of beer. It hit with a loud thud at his feet. I want to know why that's so damn funny.

It's nothing, Bessie said, clearly tickled.

Oh, Alice said, it's no big deal. Is it, Bes? We were just sitting here, waiting and drinking and watching the basketball game.

Steve looked at the TV and saw a helicopter shot of some snow-covered mountains and a vast white desert of glaciers.

Honey, Bessie said, we were talking about that phase you went through a while back.

Phase? he said. What phase?

Your mountain man phase, Alice said and burst out in laughter.

Beside tried not to join her, but she couldn't help it and started to giggle. I'm sorry, she said, they were showing the woods on TV and it just sort of came up.

Harris turned on his heels and walked back outside, the champagne bottle in tow. Steve went to follow him, but Bessie said it'd be best to give him a chance to cool off.

He gets like this, she said. He's no better than a little boy when he gets in a huff.

In a few minutes Steve heard the garage open again and saw Harris walk out carrying an axe. Steve and the women moved into the kitchen and watched out the window as Harris took a slug of the champagne, rolled up his sleeves, and swung the axe into the side of a walnut tree near the edge of their property. The sound was loud, even in the kitchen, and Bessie looked terrified.

Oh god, she said, he's going to wake up the whole neighborhood.

Three swings later and a few of the houses lit up. Bessie ran outside and yelled at him from the carport, but he wouldn't stop or even slow down. Within ten minutes all the surrounding houses were up and someone yelled that they were about to call the cops.

Before that happened Alice grabbed Steve's hand and tried to pull him away. Steve wanted to watch though. From where he was he could see everything: the sweat on Harris' brow, the glint of the axe in motion, the sharp white glow of the tree's wound. He wanted to watch until Harris was either drug away or the tree fell, but Alice was persistent.

When they got home Steve milled about the kitchen while she went upstairs to get ready for bed. He made a drink and leaned across their counter. The sink was nearby and he turned on the water and let it run. He watched it closely as it streamed down the drain. A little later he turned it off, threw back the last of his drink, and climbed the stairs.

Sitting on the bed, he untied his boots and slipped off his socks and pants. Next was his shirt and as that came over his head he was aware that it was soaked with sweat. He brought it to his face and inhaled the sour smell before balling it up and dropping it to the floor.

He couldn't get to sleep right off because he kept expecting the phone to ring. It would be Harris, calling from the county jail and looking for bail money. Steve crunched the numbers in his head. They'd have enough, or at least close to enough, if the call came.

You awake? Alice said to him.

Yeah, he answered.

Some night, she said.

Some night, he said back.

I'll tell you something about Harris, she said.

What? he said.

He waited for her to say something else, for her to have something to add to the subject, but she drifted into an easy sleep and left him alone to listen to her breathing.

After some time he settled in himself and pulled the covers up and tried to go under. But it wasn't easy. Whenever he got close he'd get the feeling he was falling, like he did when he was younger. Each time he'd nearly jump out of the bed.

Only it wasn't falling, he decided as he lay there, the morning sun starting to creep into the world. It was something else. More like there was a set of teeth somewhere, sharp and uncaring, and they were ready, at a moment's notice, to spring shut.

✪ JUST LIKE THAT ✪

TY OPENED the door to let Helen in and said, What the hell took you so long?

Oh god, she said. Ty. I just had the worst hour of my life.

Me too. I was here, waiting on you.

There was a wreck, she said. Over on the loop. I was behind the guy. I was right behind him and this truck ran a light and t-boned him. Oh my god, it was so horrible, Ty. So, so, so horrible.

No shit? he said. Do much damage?

It killed him Ty, she said. Just like that, she said and snapped her fingers.

Ty sat down at the kitchen table. He scratched at the stubble on his chin like he was considering the whole situation. Goddamn.

I know, she said and set her purse on the table. It was like lightning, I tell you. One second I was behind him and looking at his car and the next that truck ran the light and killed him.

Say, Ty said. Did you get the stuff?

My god, Helen shouted. I'm sitting here telling you something important.

Shit, he said. It's a reasonable question.

One second I'm back looking at all his stickers––

Stickers?

He had those stickers, she said. Political ones. Vote and all that. And my child is an honor student. Those kinds of stickers.

I hate those stickers, Ty said.

That's an awful thing to say. That's just an awful thing to say, Ty.

Well, he said, I hate those damn stickers. I don't know where people get off.

You and your opinions, she said. You got an opinion about everything.

I do, he said. Pay me a dollar, pour me a drink, and I might tell you some.

I parked, she said, changing the subject, and the cops came. I watched them pull that poor guy out of his car and put him in the ambulance.

Was he dead right there? Ty asked.

He was.

Then why use an ambulance?

Jesus christ, she said. Try and have some goddamn tact. I swear Ty, you've gotten mean. You've just gotten rotten this last year.

It's an ambulance, he said. Tact? C'mon, Helen. Ambulances are there to rush people to the hospital. I'm not saying anything fucking revolutionary here. They got hearses for bodies.

Bodies, she said.

142

It's about tax money, he said.

Ty, she said, you don't pay taxes.

He nodded and said, But if I did I'd be outraged. He leaned out of his chair and opened the fridge. There's nothing to drink, he said.

That's all you worry about. Can't pick up groceries, can't go look for a job, can't even sit here and listen to something awful that happened to me less than an hour ago. Worthless.

Fuck you, he said. You're a real sight tonight. A real piece of work.

Me? she said. Look at your sorry ass. You haven't even showered.

I showered, he said.

Bullshit, she said and went to the cabinet to get a glass. She filled it with water from the tap and took a long and healthy drink. You're wearing the same shirt you wore yesterday.

Ty plucked his shirt and brought it to his nose. It's clean enough, he said. Don't mean I didn't take a shower.

She left him sitting at the kitchen table and walked out of the room. When she'd disappeared he smelled himself, his arms, his hands, even lifted his feet and inhaled deeply. There was no smell even though he hadn't washed in two days. She got upset about that, for some reason, even if he didn't stink the house up. When he was done smelling himself he waited for her to come back. Five minutes passed and he thought he heard her talking in the bedroom. Probably on the phone with her sister. He lifted himself out of his chair and got down on his knees in front of the sink. Inside the cabinet down there, past the drainpipes and in a hidden corner in the back, he found the small bottle of Dark Eyes he hid for rough times. He took one drink, two, three, and replaced it.

He crossed the kitchen and the living room and walked into the hallway leading to the bedroom. She was there all right and from where he stood he could tell that she was definitely on the phone with her sister Natalie. The pair of them were thick as thieves and not above talking bad about him. He put his ear to the door and listened.

I don't know, he heard Helen say, but he had a child. Can you imagine how his wife feels? To lose somebody like that?

Huh, Ty thought. What was the use of getting so upset about a stranger? She didn't know him, didn't even know his name. Then he wondered if maybe a policeman or paramedic had given it to her. He thought of Helen hearing that name and felt hot with jealousy.

He knocked hard on the door to the bedroom.

What? she said

He looked in and said, Did you get the stuff or not?

Goddamn it, she said. Yes, all right, I got your goddamn booze.

Good, he said. You lock your car?

She fished her keys out of her purse and threw them at Ty. They hit the wall after he ducked away and landed on the carpet. There you go, she said and sighed violently.

After the door was closed he stood and listened a little while longer. This time he heard her say, I swear Natalie, he's a pig.

144

Ty took the keys and walked out to the driveway. Helen's LeBaron was parked next to his broken-down Camaro. It was still cooling down, the engine knocking around and settling. After unlocking the door he reached across and grabbed the handle of Smirnoff lying in the passenger seat.

When he picked it up he saw a slip of paper crumpled under it. He grabbed it and held it up to the streetlight. It was a receipt from the liquor store and the name TIMOTHY BUSKIRK was scrawled on the back in Helen's hurried handwriting. For a moment Ty wondered whose name it was and then he knew. With his free hand he crumpled the slip of paper and threw it as far into the weeds as he could before twisting off the cap and making his way back to the house, saying to himself, Just Like that, as he climbed the steps.

IN ALL
✪ THEIR SQUALOR ✪

HE STOOD WAITING at the door. It'd been a long week and he needed something to make him feel better. A friend said he knew a girl, she traveled in his circles, and she would do a lot of things for very little money. That's what he needed right then considering there were a lot of things he wanted to do and he had very little money.

It was night and he'd spent all of his day lounging around his apartment and taking stock of the things his wife had broken. There were the plates in the kitchen. The shower. Half a set of golf clubs snapped over her knee. The glass TV screen. Most of his record collection. Every single picture that had hung on their walls. It all sat in a depressing pile in the living room floor. His cat, named Trash Cat, weaved through the pile and investigated thoroughly.

Hey Trash Cat, he said. Take anything you want.

Trash Cat meowed.

I know that meow, he said. You want a drink.

He pulled Trash Cat up by the scruff of his neck and carried him into the kitchen. It looked nearly as bad as the living room. The dishes that hadn't been broken were piled high in the sink. He sat Trash Cat on the counter and turned the water on. Trash Cat purred, nuzzled under the dripping water, and slurped away.

That better? he asked Trash Cat.

There was a knock at the door. He went and looked out the peephole. There was no telling who it could have been. It could have been the girl and it could have been his wife, ready to cause more damage. For all he knew, it could have been the police or any number of collection agents. But he could see through the peephole that it was the girl.

Hey, he said to her, letting her in. How're you?

The girl came in and took a look around. She saw the pile in the living room and shot him a confused glance. What happened in here?

Marriage, he said, leading her over to the couch, which he'd made sure to clear off. You don't have to worry about that, he said. I think it's safe.

Safe? she said, sliding her purse off her shoulder and placing it on an end table.

Safe, he said. He looked at her. She wasn't overly pretty, but she was pretty nonetheless. You're pretty, he said.

Easy there, Romeo, she said and laughed. You're Wilkes' friend, right?

I am Wilkes' friend, he said. Yes, ma'am.

And he told you my situation? she said.

No, he said, not entirely. He just said you were hard up.

That's a way of putting it, she said.

He handed her a twenty-dollar bill, one of two he had in his wallet. It represented half of all the money he had in the entire world. The girl took the bill and tucked it into her purse at her feet. Once it was put away she took off the blouse she was wearing and pulled off her jeans. Then she undressed him and let him finish undressing her. They had sex there on the couch for the better part of fifteen minutes. At one point, Trash Cat came to investigate and rubbed his head against the girl's naked ankle.

What's his name? the girl said, shooing him away.

Trash Cat, he said. Should I put him up?

Nah, she said. That's okay.

They finished having sex and the two of them got dressed again.

Would you like something to drink? he said to her. I've got half a bottle of wine. A beer or two.

Sure, the girl said. I'll have something.

He walked into the kitchen and looked in the refrigerator. On the top shelf was the half-bottle of wine and two beers, one of them opened. He grabbed the open one for himself and got the other for the girl. She took it from him in the living room and took a long, healthy pull off it.

You don't have to worry, she said to him. I haven't been doing this for long. It's my situation.

What's your situation? he said to her.

Do you really want to know? she said.

No, he said. I'm not sure I do.

Well, she said. It's not permanent. In a month or so I'll be perfectly respectable again.

Okay, he said.

She took a sip from her beer and looked at the pile in the floor. You're married? she said.

Not for long, he said.

Oh, she said. Whose fault? she said.

Everybody's, he said.

That seemed to answer her question.

Hey, he said. I've got a record player. Want me to put on some music?

Sure, she said.

He went over to the pile and searched for what records his wife hadn't broken. There weren't many. One was a classical record with all kinds of symphonies and sonatas. He liked that one just fine, but it didn't seem appropriate for the situation. There were a couple of rock n roll ones, but they weren't by the original bands. There was Satisfaction, but it wasn't sung by The Stones. There was Hey Jude, but it wasn't by The Beatles.

I don't have much, he said to her. This one here is pretty crummy, but I can play it.

Sure, she said. Whatever.

He put on the record and Satisfaction played. It was by a band that sort of sounded like The Stones, but both of them could tell the difference.

That's not The Stones, she said. Is it?

Nope, he said. I don't think it is.

Can I get a drink of water? she said.

Sure, he said. Kitchen's right over there.

She disappeared in the kitchen and a few seconds

later she yelled for him.

What's going on? he said, walking in there.

Look, she said, pointing at the sink. Trash Cat was on the counter, drinking from the tap. I didn't know if he was supposed to be up here.

Why not? he said to her. He turned the water up for Trash Cat and gave him a pet. It's just water.

Okay, she said. That makes sense. I guess, back when I was little, our cats weren't allowed up on things.

Why not? he said.

I don't know, she said. Guess it was just a rule. Mom said they were disgusting.

Well, he said, Trash Cat deserves as good a water as anybody.

Sure he does, she agreed.

Reaching around Trash Cat, she grabbed a glass out of the sink and maneuvered it under the stream of water. Trash Cat stopped his drinking long enough to let her.

He's a good cat, she said.

He's a real good cat, he said.

With her drink of water in hand, the two of them went back into the living room and sat on the couch. They looked at the pile.

My situation, she said. It's really not permanent.

Okay, he said, reaching for his wallet again.

✪ THE EXTRA MILE ✪

IT STARTED in the morning as Hannah was leaned over in the tub and shaving her leg. She was swiping the head of her razor over her skin in an almost careless way. Her husband Brinson was brushing his teeth by the sink when the phone rang in the other room.

I'm just tired of all these calls, he said, pausing his brush. It's these telemarketers, always looking to bother you and try and sell you something. I'm done talking with them, he said.

Brinson, Hannah said, your nose is bleeding.

He turned slowly, as if he didn't believe her, and looked in the mirror.

Hannah finished her leg and rinsed it off with a quick jet of water. She stepped out of the tub, wrapped herself in a towel, and joined her husband by the mirror. In the reflection she could see a single red line of blood dripping out of his left nostril.

Sonuvabitch, Brinson said.

Here, Hannah said, pulling a piece of toilet paper,

put this on it and lean your head back.

I know how it works, Brinson said, taking the toilet paper from Hannah and pressing it against his nostril.

He leaned his head back. This isn't my first nosebleed, he said. Used to get them all the time when I was little.

All right then, Hannah said. You're the expert.

He said, No, I didn't mean it like that. Sorry. Just got creeped out there for a second.

It's fine, Hannah said and walked out of the bathroom and into their bedroom. She dropped the towel on the floor and got dressed for work by the closet. A few seconds later Brinson came in with the tissue still pressed against his nose. Has it not quit yet? Hannah said.

I'll be damned, Brinson said. It's getting worse.

He removed the tissue and Hannah could see it was already saturated with blood. The nosebleed had increased, the line of blood seemingly doubled in size and speed. Oh honey, Hannah said, that looks bad.

Don't I know it? Brinson said and put the tissue back in place.

For the next half hour the nosebleed continued and Brinson moved back and forth from whatever room Hannah was in to the bathroom, and he'd reemerge with a new fistful of tissue. When she reached for her keys on the nail by the door Brinson stopped her.

Honey, he said to her, should I go to the doctor? I mean, I can't go to work like this.

I don't know, Hannah said. She didn't know if nosebleeds were that serious. She tried to remember a time when her nose had bled, but couldn't. Do you think you should go to the doctor?

I guess not, Brinson said and sighed. He looked at the floor. Can you do me a favor? he said.

Okay, Hannah said. But I have to get ready to go.

I know, Brinson said, but can you call me in? I mean, I guess I could, but I'd rather you did it.

Brinson, Hannah said, you can call yourself in.

He raised his head from the floor and when he did Hannah could see the tissue he had was soaked through like the others before it. The look in his eyes was pitiful.

Please? he said.

When she dialed the numbers to Brinson's work a man picked up and asked who she needed to talk to. I don't know, she said. My husband's sick and he can't come to work today.

There was the sound of the man shuffling papers. Who is it? the man said.

Peter Brinson, Hannah said.

What's the problem? the man said.

He's got a nosebleed, she said.

The man coughed and said, He's got a nosebleed?

Yeah, she said. And then, It's a bad one, I guess.

He's got a bad nosebleed, the man said. You guess.

That's right, she said and looked at the clock on the stove. She was already running late. You've got that down? she said into the phone.

I've got it down, the man said.

Good, she said. Goodbye.

Brinson was standing a few feet away and when she hung up the phone he looked at her with wide eyes. What did they say? he said.

They said all right, she said. I don't know.

All right, Brinson said. Thank you, honey. That was great of you. I mean, I feel crummy. Just about as bad as I've felt in a long time. You get to work. You're already late, honey. You get to work and I'm just going to camp out on the couch until this sucker lays off.

She leaned in to give him their customary kiss goodbye, but as she grew closer to him all she could see was the bloody tissue. She pulled back. Okay, she said. Get feeling better.

Sure thing, he said, the phone starting to ring again. You have a good day, honey.

After fighting through traffic Hannah got to the lawyer's office where she worked as a receptionist. The clock in her car told her she was already six minutes late. She gathered her purse and keys and ran across the parking lot and in the door. By the time she sat down behind her desk she was covered in a light sweat.

Morning Hannah, her boss Mr. Brown said, peeking out his door.

Morning Mr. Brown, she said. She pressed the button on her phone that turned off the automated message. Sorry I'm late.

It's fine, he said. Everything all right?

Oh, she said, yeah, everything's fine. Peter had a nosebleed this morning.

A nosebleed? Mr. Brown said. He got a nosebleed?

She nodded. He was just brushing his teeth and it just started.

How about that? Mr. Brown said.

The phone rang and Mr. Brown was quick to duck back into his office. Hannah answered the call and said, Theodore Brown, Attorney-At-Law.

Hey honey, came Brinson's voice. I'm glad you made it in.

Brinson, Hannah said, what're you calling me for?

It's this nosebleed, he said. It's driving me nuts. I'm just pacing around the goddamned house. I've got my head tilted back and I'm just staring at the ceiling. I'm telling you, I've never paid so much goddamn attention to the ceiling before.

Hannah took a deep breath. Do you need anything? she said.

No, Brinson said. I guess not. Just thought maybe I'd call. I'm frustrated, honey.

Well, she said, just try and sit still. It's just a nosebleed.

You're right, Brinson said. I mean, you're really dead-on, honey. I'm going to go and lie down. Maybe that'll do the trick.

Hannah hung up the phone after saying goodbye and got to work sorting through paperwork. There were bills to send out, bills to pay, and she divided the invoices into two separate piles. When that was done she filed them into folders and labeled them to stay on top of things. Those would be her afternoon task and it was important to compartmentalize tasks because the office was very slow most of the time. Mr. Brown was not the best lawyer in town and barely made barely enough to keep her employed.

Next, Hannah did what she did most mornings when she was trying to pass time and logged onto her computer. She checked her mail and her messages and then the news. When that lost its entertainment, she typed in the address she had gotten so accustomed to. It was a video for a Ford dealership the next town over. The man who owned it was named Tex Winters, Hannah's high school boyfriend.

She'd first seen the video when a friend of hers named Val forwarded it to her a few months before. Val had said, Get a load of what Tex has been up to, and then Hannah and her had traded a few sarcastic remarks about how embarrassing the whole thing was. But Hannah couldn't help but watch the video time and time again.

Come on down to Tex Winters Ford Automotive, Tex said into the camera. He was wearing a white tank top, running shoes, running shorts, a red headband wrapped around his forehead. It was an outfit she was used to seeing on him as he'd been an all-state track and field star when they dated. The scene then cut to him running full-speed across the lot of the dealership and jumping over a quick succession of hurdles. His form was perfect and the leaps he took masterful. When he was done he looked into the camera again and wiped invisible sweat from his brow. We'll jump any hurdle, he said, to get you into your dream car.

Hannah paused the video then. Tex's handsome face stalled in a healthy grin. She looked at him and felt, all at once, a combination of nothing and everything. He was a stranger now, but she could still remember how it had been to be near him, to feel his strong body atop hers, to feel his breath in her ear. Once, after a track meet, she'd gone home with him, still clad in his uniform, and made love on his parents' couch. Looking at him, a grown man in the same uniform, she was both confused and exhilarated.

The phone rang again and shook her out of her thought. For some reason, she guiltily clicked off of the video of Tex before picking up the phone. Hello, she said. Then adding, Theodore Brown, Attorney-At-Law.

Oh god, Brinson groaned. It got worse.

Damn it, Hannah said into the phone. Brinson, she said, you can't keep calling me like this. I'm at work. Don't you understand what that means?

I do, Brinson said. I do, for sure. I'm sorry, honey. I'm just so mixed up over this nosebleed.

Well, Hannah said, that's fine, but you need to leave me alone. Do you understand that? she said.

I understand, Brinson said with a sad tinge to his voice.

Tell me you understand that you can't keep calling, Hannah said.

I understand, Brinson said. I understand that I can't keep calling.

Good, Hannah said. If it gets worse then go to the doctor. Okay?

Okay, Brinson said.

She hung up and took a long and angry breath. As she released it the door to the office opened and a small, frail-looking old woman came inside, wearing a faded blue dress and a pair of dirty tennis shoes. Is this the lawyer's? she said to Hannah.

Yes it is, Hannah said. Theodore Brown. Do you have an appointment? she asked, knowing there were no appointments that day or the next.

No, the old woman said and plopped into a chair. But I was hoping I could talk to the lawyer.

Okay, Hannah said and got up from her desk and

walked toward Mr. Brown's door. Just get comfortable and I'll see if we can make that happen.

Yes ma'am, the old woman said.

Hannah knocked on Mr. Brown's door and then heard him say to come in. She opened it and found him in his usual position——legs up on his desk, his arm throwing a blue racquetball against the wall to his side over and over again. There's someone here who wants to see you, Hannah said after closing the door behind her.

Who is it? he said, catching the ball and pausing.

Hannah said, An older woman. She doesn't have an appointment.

Ah hell, Mr. Brown said and drug his feet off his desk. He opened a drawer and put away the ball. He straightened his tie. Bring her in, he said. Fuck it.

Hannah returned to the reception area and told the woman she could go in. The woman took her time navigating the few feet from her chair into Mr. Brown's office. Every few seconds she'd stop in her tracks to gather her breath. After what seemed like an eternity she reached for the knob and disappeared inside.

For the next twenty minutes Hannah sat and ruffled needlessly through the remaining papers on her desk. There was nothing to do, no task until that afternoon. She thought of Brinson and his nosebleed and it made her shudder. She wondered why people got nosebleeds and she got on the computer again. A quick search later and she was reading through all the possible causes. Some were small and meaningless, others terrifying.

She clicked off the page about nosebleeds and typed Tex's name into the search bar. She found the video she'd already watched a few dozen times and with it was another video she hadn't seen. It was pretty much the same ad––Tex in his uniform––but this time he was running laps on an actual track. Hannah recognized it as the one at the high school, where Tex had won so many of his awards.

As he finished his workout, Tex looked into the camera and smiled. We'll go the extra mile, he said, to get you into the car of your dreams.

Hannah instantly thought of a race she'd seen Tex run their junior year of high school. It'd been the 1500 Meter in Sectionals and Tex's rival, a long and gaunt boy from Sullivan, ran the next lane over. Hannah had sat in the stands with Tex's mother Dorothy and as they'd neared the final stretch, neck and neck, she had reached over and grasped Hannah's hand. She remembered how she'd felt right then, Hannah did, Tex striding in the fading afternoon sun, that other boy falling quickly behind, Dorothy's hand getting tighter and tighter in her own, the whole thing, the whole picture, growing clearer and clearer.

She had thought, with great clarity, This is my future.

Sitting in her chair behind her desk, Hannah could still feel the warmth from the sun, the pressure in her hand. She felt herself smiling, and then noticed the button flashing on her phone. It was Mr. Brown's signal to join him in his office. Hannah picked up her notepad and a pen.

Mrs. Brinson, Mr. Brown said, won't you sit and take notes for the duration of my meeting with Ms. White?

Absolutely, Hannah said and sat in the chair next to the old woman. She smiled at her and then pressed the tip of her pen against the paper. All ready when you are, she said.

All right, Mr. Brown said. Ms. White, if you would, please start your story over from the beginning. Mrs. Brinson here is simply going to jot it all down for further reference.

Sure, the old woman said. I was just telling Mr. Brown here that my good-for-nothing son took off a few weeks ago with my car and I've got to do something about it.

Good, Mr. Brown said. Could you state, for the record, your son's name?

Harold, she said. Harold White. And don't get me wrong, I love him to death. Just love him to death. But sooner or later you got to open your eyes and see what a person's like. You got to look through all that love and get down to the meat of it.

Okay, Mr. Brown said. And what's the situation with your son?

Oh, the old woman said and settled in her seat. Harry's been no good for a long time. Since he was a teenager. Used to get in fights and smoke dope with his friends. He was drinking by the age of sixteen.

That's all fine, Mr. Brown said, but what's the current situation?

Is she getting all this? the old woman said and pointed at Hannah.

I am, Hannah said. No worries.

She's fine, Mr. Brown said. Go on, Ms. White.

What I'm trying to say, Ms. White said, is that

Harry's been taking my money for as long as I can remember. It was a few bucks here, a few bucks there. He'd get in my purse and help himself to whatever there was. And I let that go on a little too long, Mr. Brown. I should've stomped that out the first time I ever noticed. But I'm his mom. You got to understand that.

Mr. Brown said, I do.

And I guess all that adds up, the old woman said. Cause I got up a few weeks ago, made my coffee, had some breakfast, and when I looked out the window at my carport I saw that my car was gone. Now, I don't drive anymore, but that's not the point, Mr. Brown. It's the principle of the matter.

It is, Mr. Brown said.

Hannah wrote THE PRINCIPLE OF THE MATTER on her notepad and underlined it for good measure.

The old woman huffed and said, Now he's down in Kentucky. I know just where he's at, Mr. Brown. Got the address and everything. She reached into her purse and pulled out a crumpled piece of paper. Berea, Kentucky, she said. He's even called and said he was sorry. Said he'd met some woman and they'd run off. Even said he was gonna pay me back for the car. But I haven't seen a check since. You tell me what a mom's supposed to do, Mr. Brown. Because I've prayed and prayed about this and I just don't know.

Hannah, having worked for Mr. Brown for two years, knew how these matters worked. Mr. Brown wanted nothing else written down but the necessary pieces of information. He had told Hannah, many times over, that clients liked nothing better than to go on and on about their plights and misfortunes. They want a lawyer, he'd said to her once before, but they want that lawyer to be a psychologist too. Just write down what matters and leave out all the junk, he'd said.

So Hannah quit taking notes after getting down the important parts. She sat there in her chair while the old woman went on about what a disappointment her son had been and all the heartache he'd caused. She sat there and nodded her head, drawing her pen close enough to the paper to make it seem as if she was taking notes, but never made another mark. In her two years Hannah had learned how to switch off like a lamp when clients got to rambling.

Instead of listening, she let her mind wander. Again, she thought of Brinson and pictured him lying on the couch, tissue pressed against his nose. But the more she thought about it the worse the nosebleed got and she was imagining it growing out of control and covering Brinson and the couch and then the room with blood. That was too much, so she backed out of that thought and found herself on Tex again. The couch that Brinson had been lying on with his nosebleed turned into the couch she and Tex shared after his meet. She was remembering how he'd felt, how he'd smelled, how he'd tasted of dried sweat when Mr. Brown got her attention again.

I think we're good, he said to her. Hannah noticed he and the old woman were staring at her, the latter with a sense of confusion. Okay, Hannah said. Good.

She carried her notepad back to her desk, where the message light was blinking on the phone. She picked up the receiver, pressed the button, and listened.

It was Brinson. Hannah, this thing won't go away.

I've been doing everything I can. Laying down, laying my head back. I looked in a book and it said to pinch your nose, but that only made it worse. Work called and left a message. I guess I've got to meet with the head honcho tomorrow. Jesus, he said. I'm going out of my mind here.

Hannah pressed the delete button and waited for the next message. It was Brinson. Again.

Honey, he said, it's not slowing down. What if I'm dying? What if this is it? Do nosebleeds kill people? I mean, you only have so much blood. Right? I wish I could hear your voice. I bet you're busy. I'm sorry, he said. I just wanted to hear your voice.

She pressed delete before he finished and sat at her desk.

A nosebleed, she said to herself.

The old woman came out of the office a little while later and hobbled out the front door. She stopped before she did and gave Hannah a strange look. She didn't say goodbye, or thank you, just opened the door and disappeared outside. Mr. Brown wasn't far behind and he peeked out from his office and said to Hannah, Hey, you all right?

I'm fine, she said.

You sure? he said.

Sure, she said.

Okay, he said.

Okay, she said.

She wasted no time then diving into the bills and invoices in the folders. She wrote checks and addressed the letters going out. She finished all of that within a half hour and sat there at her desk with nothing else to do. She got on the computer but had no desire to look at anything. So she logged off and knocked on Mr. Brown's door.

Come in, he said.

She popped her head in and saw him with his legs up on the desk. He was throwing the ball against the wall and catching it. I'm not feeling so hot, she said. The schedule's empty the rest of the day. You care if I head home?

Mr. Brown caught his ball and looked at it. Sure, he said without much feeling. Get better.

I will, she said.

After gathering her purse she went outside and got in her car. She turned the engine over and looked at the time. Twelve-thirty five. It was still early. She knew she could drive home, but the thought of it made her sick. She'd spend the rest of the day taking care of Brinson and listening to him complain about his damned bloody nose.

Instead, she drove to a nearby pharmacy store and walked inside. She went straight to the cosmetics aisle and bought some mascara, eye shadow, lipstick. They were all shades she hadn't worn in years. Ones that were too bright or dramatic. She paid for them and went back to the car. In the rearview mirror she painted her eyes dark and her eyelashes thick. The lipstick, a strong shade of red, framed her mouth.

The drive to Tex Winters Ford Automotive was a little under twenty minutes, but it took longer for Hannah because she kept losing her nerve and pulling over into different gas stations to reconsider. Each time she did, three in total, she'd give herself a pep talk in the rearview mirror.

Come on, she said to herself. You only live once.

Or, What's the problem? You're just going to say hello.

But when she looked in the mirror she saw herself painted in the makeup and knew she was lying. The fantasy had already started to take shape. She was going to find Tex at the dealership and pretend to be in the market for a new car. They'd catch up, fire up the old flame, and maybe go for a test drive. Already Hannah could see herself in some cut-rate hotel room, Tex huffing and puffing on top of her like the old days.

Eventually she pulled into the parking lot for Tex Winters Ford Automotive. There was a field of cars, their prices marked on their windshields, streamers and banners emitting from the top of the office and zipping to the four corners of the lot. Next to the entrance was a cardboard cutout of Tex, decked out in his track and field uniform, a dialogue balloon hanging above him that said, We'll Go The Extra Mile.

Hannah pushed open the door to the dealership and was hit instantly by a wall of cold air. She shivered and looked around. There was a blue minivan parked in the center of the building and behind it a group of desks and cubicles. A heavyset man wearing a blue windbreaker was already approaching her and plying on his salesman's grin.

Can I do you for? he said.

Hi, Hannah said, looking around. Is Tex here?

Huh, the man said. I think maybe he is. I can help you out with whatever you need though.

No, Hannah said. Tex and I are old friends. Could

you let him know there's someone here to see him?

The heavyset man cocked his head and looked Hannah over like he wasn't quite sure what to make of her. Sure, he said. Be right back.

He disappeared past the desks and left Hannah by herself to look over the minivan on display. It was sharp, a dark shade of blue, the interior leather, the whole thing tricked out with chrome and all the bells and whistles. On the front windshield somebody had written, in a starburst, Perfect For A Family Or Just For A Cruise.

Can I help you? came a voice.

Hannah turned and saw Tex standing on the other side of the minivan, wearing a red polo shirt that had the dealership's name on the breast. He looked healthy and fit. The boy she'd known grown into his full frame. Tex, Hannah said. Hello.

Hey, Tex said. Walt told me you wanted to see me?

Hannah circled around the minivan and reached out to shake Tex's hand. It was strong, though Hannah could tell he was sparing her his full grip. It's Hannah, she said.

Hannah, Tex said. He looked at her. Hannah, he said again, finally placing her. It's you?

It's me, she said with a laugh. You got it.

Oh god, Tex said, smiling broadly. Hannah, I can't believe you're standing here. My god. It's so good to see you.

He held out his arms and she flung herself into his hug. It's so good to see you too, she said in his embrace.

Holy shit, he said as he let go. What're you doing here? How are you? I'm sorry, he said, I'm just so surprised to see you.

Yeah, she said. I'm fine. I just saw your ad on TV.

Oh no, Tex said and feigned embarrassment. Then, just as quickly, he adopted the pose he'd struck in the video and pointed at Hannah. We'll go the extra mile, he said in his TV voice, to get you in the car of your dreams.

That's right, she said, laughing. That's the one.

That's terrible, he said. I should've known that was going to come back to bite me.

No, she said. No, no, no. I thought it was charming.

He said, Well, it's something. That's for sure.

They stood laughing awkwardly for a moment and Hannah took the chance to look down at Tex's left hand. She saw a plain gold ring on his finger and felt her stomach churn. So, she said, feeling deflated, what's new with you?

Oh, he said, you know. Got this business. Just trying to hustle and keep the lights on.

I see, Hannah said. Wife? Kids and a dog running in the yard?

Yep, he said and lifted that left hand up as if he were admitting some kind of guilt. Got a ball and chain and a couple of rugrats.

That's good, Hannah said. That's really good.

Sure, Tex said. It sure is. How about you?

Hannah thought of Brinson then and saw him bleeding on the couch. Yeah, she said weakly.

Well all right then, Tex said. Look at us all grown up.

No doubt, Hannah said.

Speaking of, he said, you come in here to catch up

or to look at a motor vehicle? If you came to chat we could go grab some lunch.

No, Hannah said without thinking and then lied, I came for a car.

Oh, Tex said. Okay. What kind?

Hannah quickly turned her head and looked at the minivan in the showroom. This one, she said. This minivan.

It's a good one, Tex said. That's for sure. Pretty good deal on it too.

All right, Hannah said. I like it.

Tell you what, Tex said, let's take her for a spin. You're going to fall in love with this baby.

Sure, Hannah said. Let's do it.

Tex excused himself then and walked into the back to get the keys. Hannah stood and waited nervously by the minivan while the other salesman, stationed at their bullpens just off the showroom floor, watched her. When Tex reappeared, keys in hand, she forced herself to smile.

Ready to give her a run? Tex said.

You bet, Hannah said.

She got into the minivan's driver's seat and waited for Tex to slide in. As he did Hannah heard the rumbling of an ancient-sounding motor overhead. The wall in front of her started to lift like a garage door and she could see out into the lot and the highway just past it.

All right, Tex said. Let's get going.

Hannah put the minivan into drive and slowly rolled out of the showroom.

You've got everything you need in here, Tex said,

reaching for the buttons on the console. All your music and navigation. I mean, he said, this thing's fully loaded.

Hannah turned onto the highway and merged with traffic. The minivan felt good to drive, smooth and comfortable. Tex turned through the stations on the radio and found one that was playing something by The Stone Temple Pilots. It had been his favorite band in high school and Hannah had spent many a day and night listening to their albums while the two of them kissed and sweated together.

Now that's an oldie but a goodie, Tex said.

Down the road Hannah realized she was feeling better. She had left Brinson, the office, Mr. Brown, behind, if only for a while. It was one forty-seven in the afternoon and she was miles from anywhere she would've normally been. She felt lighter. She looked in the passenger seat and saw a grinning, glowing Tex.

How's she feel? he said.

Couldn't be better, Hannah said.

I tell you, Tex said, it's a dream to drive. That's for sure. It's got all the gadgets and things you'd want. And let me tell you something. Most of these minivans are pretty pathetic. They're no fun to cart around, that's for sure. But this one? he said. It's a fine looking automobile. Just what a beautiful woman like yourself should be driving.

Hannah looked again at Tex, who was still grinning. It was the look he'd given her all those times when he'd had something in mind.

I got an idea, Hannah said. Let's just drive off. You and me. We'll just skip this podunk town and head for

169

hills.

Tex laughed. Yeah, he said. That's the ticket. Just drive west and start over.

That's what I'm saying, Hannah said. Hit an ATM and get a bunch of cash and start over.

Hasta la vista, Tex said.

Hasta la vista, Hannah said and laughed. She felt a sudden burst of confidence and reached across the leather console. She touched Tex's leg and felt the taut muscle beneath his khakis. Sounds pretty good, she said.

Tex immediately sat up straight in the passenger seat and moved his leg from her touch. Uh, he said, Hannah, we ought to bring this baby back to the dealership. We're getting a little far out.

What about driving west? she said, gripping the wheel with both hands now. What about starting over?

C'mon, Tex said, looking down at his lap. C'mon, Hannah.

Hannah didn't say anything. She waited for the next chance to turn around and headed back in the direction of the dealership. A few minutes of silence later, she pulled back into the parking lot and near the still-open door.

This is fine, Tex said reaching for his door handle. I'll have the guys get it back in place.

Sure, Hannah said. She turned the engine off and removed the keys. I'm going to have to think about it some, she said.

Tex stepped down onto the lot. Yeah, you should probably talk to your husband about it.

I probably should, Hannah said.

170

After giving the keys back to Tex Hannah hurriedly walked back to her car and got inside. Tex wasted no time hurrying into the dealership. She looked back to see if maybe he was watching but saw only the cardboard cutout with the dialogue balloon. We'll go the extra mile, it said.

Without turning the radio on, Hannah drove back into town and into the driveway of her house. She sat there in the car for a long while and ran through the drive with Tex over and over. She wanted to go back and stop herself from touching his leg. She wanted to go back and stop herself from driving there in the first place. She wanted to go back and stop the day from ever starting.

When she opened the front door the first thing she saw was Brinson all sprawled out on the living room couch, twisted and contorted, one of his legs hanging off the back of the couch and the other on the floor. His face was scrunched as if in agony. He was still pressing a ball of tissue against his nose while a crowd of bloodied and crumpled ones lay beside him and on the coffee table and the floor. Everywhere Hannah looked she saw bloody tissues.

Oh thank god, Brinson said, sitting up. I'm so glad you're home, honey. It's still going.

Still? Hannah said. She dropped her purse and hung her keys on the nail by the door.

I'm telling you, Brinson said, I don't think this thing's ever going to end. Come here, he said and got off the couch. She followed him into the kitchen where the table was similarly covered with tissues caked in dried blood. At the center of the table though was an open copy of an old medical textbook. It's all right here, Brinson said. I think maybe I'm cursed.

Brinson, Hannah said. I'm getting a headache.

Well, Brinson said, pulling the tissue from his nose and examining it. It was scarlet with blood and Hannah could see a new trickle making its way out of his nostril. I'm sorry, honey. I'm sorry you've got a headache. Can I tell you what I've been thinking about?

In a little while, Hannah said and walked wearily toward the bedroom. I think I'm going to lie down.

All right, Brinson said and followed her into the room. He went into the adjacent bathroom and got another stretch of tissue for his nose. You lay down, honey. Get some rest. When you get up I'll run you through it. I mean, this thing is driving me crazy. This nosebleed. I don't think it's ever gonna stop.

Hannah laid down on the bed and put her head on a pillow. It was the one Brinson usually slept on and it smelled sour like he did of the morning. All right, she said. Just give me a few minutes. Just let me rest.

She closed her eyes and tried to sleep but couldn't make herself go under. She stayed still in the blackness and listened to Brinson in the other room. She could hear the couch springs squeaking when he laid down and when he got up. She could hear him going back and forth between the living room and the kitchen. Sometimes she could even hear him frantically flipping through the thin pages of the book on the table.

Eventually sleep came and she had a quick and strange dream. She and Brinson were on a trip somewhere, maybe their honeymoon, and they were sharing a bottle of red wine and talking about the

172

future. It wasn't a place they had been though, the restaurant they were sitting in, and they had never had any conversation like it on their actual trip. Just as that thought occurred to Hannah she looked across the table at Brinson, in the dream, and watched a stream of blood the color of the wine pour of both of his nostrils.

She woke with a start when she heard the phone ringing in the other room. Brinson answered it and she listened to him speak into the receiver. No, he said, we're all fine here. We don't need anything. Then a pause where she thought she could actually hear him thinking. Listen, he said after a moment, you don't know anything about nosebleeds do you?

✪ KEEP ON KEEPING ON ✪

BACK THEN I couldn't get enough of anything. Didn't matter what it was: women, food, drink, smoke. You name it and I wanted more.

At the time I had this girl, a blind girl named Natalie. When I got tired of running around I'd go over and see her and she'd be just where I left her, parked right there on her couch and reading some book with her fingers. It was the same story every time I came around. I'd walk in the door and she'd want to jump right into bed.

Let's go to the store and pick up some groceries, I'd say. Let's spend some of that money of yours.

Her dad was a lawyer upstate and didn't have much time for her at all. Instead, he'd send her checks every month. Used to stuff them into greeting cards with bumblebees or birds on the cover. On the memo line he'd write encouraging things like Hang in there! or Do your best!

What kind of card is it this time? she'd ask.

It's a sailboat, I'd say. Or, An owl. Whatever the case was. I'd tell her and then she'd nod like she understood, even though she'd been blind since the day she was born and had never laid eyes on a sailboat or an owl.

What color is it? she'd ask.

Does it matter?

Sure.

Blue, I'd say. Every last inch of it blue.

More often than not I'd just get done telling her about one of those cards and she'd want to head to the bedroom. She was the only person I knew who had a harder time getting enough than I did. With a smile she'd lay back on the covers of her bed and say, Go on, give it to me.

And I would.

If it wasn't midnight by the time we'd finish we'd load into my car and head on over to the Kroger's. She'd hold onto the grocery cart while I scanned the shelves and read everything off to her.

They got tomatoes, I'd say. Soup.

What's on sale?

Macaroni, I'd say. Two for one.

Get three, she'd say.

You're being difficult.

She'd shoot me that smile of hers and nod. You love it, she'd say.

I really did. She was smart and funny and didn't give two shits what I did or didn't do. I could go a whole week without combing my hair and she'd just run her hands through it and smile like crazy. Expectations were low and that's just how I liked it.

Now, that's not to say I wasn't busy on the side. For

whatever reason, back then, I had some magic working for me. Made me think about a story I'd read when I was little about a boy who happened upon a lucky rabbit's foot and everything went golden for awhile. It was that easy.

What I'd do is sidle up to some girl at a bar and just ask her what her plans were for the night.

Depends, they'd say. What're yours?

Natalie didn't care one bit. I'd come over and she'd get a whiff of some perfume on my clothes and say, You know, there's nothing wrong with my sense of smell.

Oh yeah? I said. What'd you smell?

Skin-so-soft, she said. And whiskey sours.

Bingo, I said and led her back into her room.

One night, close to the end, we were lying there in her bed and it was already too late to head to Kroger's or anywhere else for that matter. The both of us were covered in sweat and pretty far tuckered out anyway. She turned to me and said, Do you think you'll ever get tired of tomcatting around?

I thought about that and considered the question. We'd never really talked about the subject before and I thought maybe she was giving me some shit. I don't know, I said, you think you'll ever get tired of being blind?

Right away I could tell the joke didn't go over well. She pulled away and covered herself with the sheet. That's a cruel thing to say, she said. A real, real cruel thing to say.

For a while I tried to apologize but then the hour got late and eventually we just sort of went to sleep. The next day was Saturday and when we got up she said she wanted to go to the store. We got there and she wanted everything on the shelves. I'd name something and she'd tell me to throw it in the cart. You never saw so many groceries in all your life.

We had a feast when we got back. I cooked up a couple of steaks on her stove with some butter and baked potatoes. There was a cheesecake she'd picked out in the frozen aisle and I sat that out to thaw while we knocked back four bottles of wine and had all the salad and green beans we could handle.

You full yet? I asked when all the food was gone.

Never, she said. Take me to bed.

In the morning I got up and fixed some eggs and biscuits and a pot of coffee. Even got a carafe full of juice and sat it on the table with a flower we'd bought from the nursery. For no good reason I took one of the cards her dad had sent——a yellow number with a train and the words Keep On Keeping On in the belly of a floating cloud——and set it out for decoration. I got us both a plate and we ate without talking. When we were near done she pushed hers out of the way and asked me to lean in.

Why? I said.

I want to touch your face.

After some protesting I did as she asked and she reached out and at first she put the tips of her fingers on my cheeks, then my forehead, then down and over my eyes and lips and chin. Then it was her palms and I felt like I was really getting worked over.

This must be what a pie feels like, I said.

Shh, she said.

Jesus, I said. Lighten up.

Let me do this, she said.

I went ahead and shut up and let her touch my face and do whatever she wanted. The whole thing went on another couple of minutes and then when she was satisfied she went got back to eating her breakfast. I cleaned up and rinsed off the dishes and then took off for the day. I had some running around to do, some bills to pay, a guy to see about a car, and some girls to attend to. As I was halfway out the door I asked her, See you tonight?

We'll see, she said.

Later I got good and loused at a place called Tim's and nearly got into it with the fella I was supposed to buy the car off of. He had his sister with him and whenever he'd go to the bathroom she'd make eyes at me or reach into my lap under the bar. One time she wasn't quick enough on the draw and he saw what was going on and liked to have slapped my jaw out of place. The only thing I knew to do was give him a good butt with the crown of my head and that knocked him to the floor. Before I could get on top of him that sister of his had her nails dug into my cheeks and was trying to pry my eyes out.

Within the hour I made the trip over to Natalie's place. At one point the car hit eighty and I had the window down and was leaning out to let the wind wipe away the blood. I pulled into her driveway not long after and stumbled up to the door. All I wanted in the world was to get in there and read one of her dad's cards to her and trip into bed and be one with her again. When I knocked on the door though there wasn't an answer.

So I knocked again.

178

The next time I started hollering, yelling, Natalie, honey, I know you ain't deaf too.

That didn't work either so I walked over to window looking into her living room and saw her sitting there on the couch, curled up and reading one of those books with her fingertips. I gave the window a couple of good thumps but that didn't make a difference either. If she heard me——and I know she had to've——she didn't let on or flinch the least little bit.

All that went on for another half hour or so until one of her neighbors leaned out his front door and told me he'd already called the cops. I told him what he could do with his cops and then figured it was best if I got to moving. When I backed out of the driveway I looked in the window again and she hadn't moved off that couch. I called the next day and the day after and the day after that and never did get through.

You got to figure, I reckon anyway, that something must've changed. Either she changed or I changed. Maybe we both changed. I don't know. Or maybe, just maybe, after all that time, she'd finally got her fill.

✪ ONE OF THOSE CALLS ✪

WHEN HE GOT good and drunk and the night wore on he liked to get on the phone and call up ex-girlfriends. He had a letter to write that evening though and so he sat down on the porch to write it before retiring to the phone. It was already dark outside at that point. Luckily he'd replaced the bulb in the porch light the week before and all it would take to get some light would be to walk inside and flip the switch. When he went in though he got sidetracked. He had to carry all his empty cans in and that led to getting another beer and that led him to the kitchen where the phone was screwed into the wall.

He looked at the ragged piece of paper on the counter with all the numbers. By this point most of his ex-girlfriends had learned to just let the phone ring. Some got angry and told him never to call again. Christine was one of the last few who would put up with him and so that was who he called.

Hello, Christine said.

Hi there, he said. It's Chappy.

Chappy, she said like she wasn't sure she knew a Chappy. How goes it?

Just fine, he said. Aces and kings.

Sure thing, Christine said. You sound drunk.

There's a mighty fine reason for that, he said.

And that is?

Because I'm drunk, he said.

Uh huh, she said.

Hey, he said. You busy, darling?

Nothing I can't finish later, she said. What can I do for you?

Well Christine, he said, I was just sitting down to write a letter and I needed to ask somebody a question. A real serious question.

If this is one of those calls, she said, I can't handle it right now. We didn't work out and that's the end of it. It's been four long years. I can't handle you crying and begging.

Okay, he said.

Okay meaning that's what you called for, or okay, you understand?

Understand, he said. Loud and clear.

Good, she said. Okay. The question.

He said, The question is important. Real important.

Okay, she said.

And I want you to answer. The truth. Nothing but.

Hell, she said. What is it, Chappy?

Well, he said, here it is. Do you think I'm some kind of terrible sonuvabitch?

What? she said.

He said, You know me pretty good, Christine.

Chappy, she said, I told you I couldn't handle one of these phone calls.

No, he said and got another beer. It's not one of those calls. He looked in the refrigerator and opened a drawer and then shut it. It's a question, he said. I need to know.

Where's this coming from?

I don't know, he said, looking at the pen and paper he'd planned on using to write the letter. They were sitting on the kitchen table next to a phonebook he'd left out in the rain. I'm writing a letter, he said, and I want to get it right.

A letter? Christine said. It's not a letter to me, is it? Cause I can't handle that either.

No ma'am, he said. Unless you want a letter.

No Chappy, she said. The last thing I want is a letter.

Okay. Well, I got a letter to write, he said, and I need to know if maybe I'm some kind of sonuvabitch. If maybe I just didn't realize it.

Christine didn't answer at first. The line went so silent he thought maybe she'd hung up. He even said Hello, you still there? and she said she was an was thinking of a way to say something.

Chappy, she said, finally, slowly, I think you're a fine person, a good one sometimes, but you can act like a real sonuvabitch.

He rolled that around in his head and took a drink of his beer and picked the pen off the pad of paper and opened the soggy phonebook. While he thought out what she'd said he ran the tip of the pen across a random page and the page ripped open like a zipper.

That's fair, he said into the phone.

I think you get lost, Christine said. You're a sweetheart most times, and I think you've got a good heart but you get lost. You set your sights on something else, she said and paused. Someone else, she said. And then you turn into a real asshole.

Right then he remembered this one time, back when Christine and him were still together, when they'd lived together, and he'd come home from a fishing trip. She'd been sitting at the same kitchen table that was in his kitchen. She was smoking and drinking a gin and tonic. He told her all about the trip and how he'd been in the boat with his friend and a storm had turned up, an electrical storm, and how lightning kept hitting the water around them.

We almost died, he told her. The real deal. We rowed like mad men to get to the shore. And the waves were crashing down and we kept getting turned around and losing track of where we were going.

She'd looked at him and took a long, stiff drink of her gin and tonic. After she'd swallowed it down she said, You asshole. Just pick a direction next time and go.

Hey, he said to her through the phone, remember when I was caught in the storm in that boat?

Sure I do, she said. I gotta go though, Chappy. Things to do.

Sure thing, he said. Hey, thanks for picking up.

No problem, she said. He heard the clink of what he figured to be ice cubes floating in a sea of McCormick's. And Chappy, she said, I should tell you. Kent proposed last month.

What'd you say? he asked.

Yes, she answered. I said yes.

Hell, he said. You're settling.

Well, she said, whatever. I don't care what you think. You don't have the right to criticize considering you never asked.

Tell you what, he said. I'm gonna catch the next flight out your way and propose.

Oh god, she said. Don't.

No, he said. I'm gonna make you say no to me.

Chappy, she pleaded.

Okay, he said. Just be ready when you hear that doorbell.

Goodnight, she said. And good luck with that letter.

When she hung up he ran upstairs and packed a suitcase and a bag for his toothpaste and deodorant and shampoo. He'd already made up his mind to get on a plane and propose to Christine, but when he got downstairs with his bags he saw the pad of paper and pen sitting on the kitchen table.

He paused. Set the bags down and got another beer out of the fridge.

Outside he sat on his porch again. Already he knew what he wanted to say in the letter, what words and phrases he wanted to use, but he didn't start right yet. He sat there in his chair and drank his beer and listened. For an hour or so it was quiet and it gave him some time to think. But then the night got darker as clouds took form. Lightning flashed in the distance and he thought, maybe, for a second, he heard thunder rolling in from behind.

✪ NEED ✪

WHEN HEADLIGHTS washed over her darkened living room Wanda got up off the couch and looked out the window to see if Dave had come back home. They lived on one of the busiest streets in town and the cars stopping at the light cattycorner from their house were always flashing them. Usually Wanda wouldn't of paid them any mind but it was getting late and her husband had been gone the better part of the night.

The way he had explained it the day before was that he had reached his fill in dealing with her ex Hank. His bullshit, and her bullshit, had tired him out. He said, unless something changed, he was going to make some calls and get the hell out of dodge.

I can't live like this, he said. That sonuvabitch is always calling and threatening and showing up drunk in the middle of the night. You either let me deal with it or else we can't be in love anymore.

Wanda was in the floor begging him at that point. She had the hem of his work shirt in her hands. But I'm in love, she said. I'm in love with you.

Well, Hank said, looking down at her, then let me handle it. We need to stop pussyfooting around with this thing. We need to get serious.

Need. Wanda thought about the word as she sat back on the couch. It seemed like something she'd heard her whole life. As a girl her mom had always said she needed this thing or that. Braces on her legs and teeth. Special classes after school for speech. A new hair-do so a boy might take her out for once.

She clicked on the TV to pass the time. The late night shows were winding down and the hosts saying their goodbyes. One of them stood in front of a band in his suit and blew the camera a big, exaggerated kiss. As the show went to credits Wanda felt hot tears rolling down her cheeks.

She wanted Dave home. She wanted him to come in smelling like he did every day after work, like sweat and sawdust, and she wanted to throw her arms around his neck and hear him say he loved her. She wanted to sit down at the table and hear him complain about his day and watch as he shoveled the food she'd made him into his mouth and as he drank his first beer of the night.

In the kitchen she opened the fridge and looked at the plate of food she'd made. It wasn't anything special, one of those boxed meals where all she had to do was add hamburger, but it was one of his favorites and she'd hoped it would help ease the tension from the conversation. The light from the fridge twinkled on the foil that covered the plate. She picked it up and peeled back the foil. The noodles and meat looked different now. Older. She put the foil back in place and then set the plate on its shelf.

Done with that, she returned to the living room and looked at the TV again. The late night show had been replaced by an infomercial. Two actors and an actress were sitting around a table filled with photo-ready plates of food. There were omelets and salads and steaks and bowls of fruit. They were talking about some amazing new invention.

The Kitchenator, Wanda heard the woman say.

What's this Kitchenator all about? the man sitting next to her asked.

Why, the woman said, smiling at the camera, the Kitchenator is the most exciting piece of culinary technology in years.

The living room lit up then with another set of headlights. Wanda got up and halfheartedly looked, but the car just drove on by. She leaned to get her cigarettes off the coffee table and pulled one from the pack. She lit it with her disposable lighter and took a pull and then cycled the smoke back out.

Are you tired of all the fuss in your kitchen? a voiceover said on the TV. Footage played of two of the actors who had been sitting at table. One of the men was working a blender and the woman was chopping onions. When the man hit a button on the blender liquid exploded out the top and covered his face and shirt. The woman went to chop with her knife and missed. She pulled her hand up to her mouth as if she'd cut herself. Are you tired of all the hoops you have to go through just to put a meal on the table? the voiceover said.

Wanda ashed her cigarette into the mouth of a coke

can and watched the commercial. The frustrated couple wiped themselves off and bandaged their wounds. They looked at each other, sighed, and then nodded.

Introducing The Kitchenator, the voiceover said. The handiest, easiest kitchen tool ever invented.

The Kitchenator appeared onscreen. To Wanda it looked like any other kitchen appliance. Words popped up next to it saying it could blend, chop, cut, process, and so much more. The couple who had had such a hard time blending and chopping were all of a sudden fixing gourmet meals and serving up course after course to crowds of satisfied-looking, beautiful friends.

The Kitchenator, the voice said again. The only kitchen tool you'll ever need.

The room was filled with light then and the glow lasted long enough that Wanda got excited. She heard what she thought to be the familiar sound of Dave's truck idling in the drive so she dropped her cigarette into the coke can and got up to look out the window. It was Dave's truck and he was stepping out onto the drive. When the door opened he came in and she could see he was tired. His white undershirt was soaked through with sweat, his hair was wet with it, and his jeans filthy with dirt and mud. At his side he carried his shotgun.

Honey, Wanda said and threw her arms around him, I'm glad you're home.

That right? he said, propping the gun up against the wall before pulling away from her and walking into the kitchen. She saw the fridge door open and him disappear behind it, only to reemerge with a beer and the plate of food.

—

Did you talk to him? she said. Did you talk to Hank?

What's that? Dave said as he put the beer and plate on the kitchen table and pulled out a chair. When he sat it was with a groan. Did I talk to Hank?

Yeah, Wanda said. Did you go and talk things out with Hank?

I did, Dave said and pulled back the foil on the plate. He reached and got a fork out of a drawer by the sink and scooped up some of the noodles and meat.

Wanda said, I can heat that up, Dave. It's not a problem.

Nah, Dave said. It's fine like this.

She watched him eat for a moment and thought to herself that he did it like he hadn't had a bite in years. From time to time he stopped long enough to run his dirty hands through his sweaty hair and put it back in place.

What did he say? she said.

What? Dave said. He grabbed his beer and tossed it back. What did Hank say?

Right, Wanda said. What did Hank say?

Not much, Dave said. Say, he said, could you do me a favor, honey?

Sure, Wanda said. No problem. You name it.

Okay, Dave said. Tell you what. Go outside and start me a fire. Get some of that wood together and start a fire the way I taught you.

Honey, Wanda said, it's one in the morning.

Doesn't matter, he said and dropped his fork on the plate. It made an awful sound. I asked you to do something.

All right, Wanda said. She went into their bedroom

and walked through the mounds of dirty clothes and trash and got a sweatshirt out of the closet and a pair of her house shoes. When she got back to the kitchen Dave was looking at the bottle of beer like he expected it to move. Honey, Wanda said. I got to ask you something.

Ask away, Dave said.

Well, she said, I just got to ask if you love me.

Do I love you? he said.

Yeah, Wanda said. You were saying yesterday we might not get to be in love anymore. And I want to be in love.

Baby, he said with a nod, we're still in love.

Good, Wanda said and went out the back door.

The backyard was dark except for the orange glow of the security light Dave had had the city put in the summer before when Hank had made a habit of showing up drunk out of his mind and threatening her and Dave. Once he'd had a revolver stuck down the front of his jeans but it wasn't like he'd reached for it. For Wanda it was clear that all he wanted to do was let her know he still loved her and wanted her back. Unlike Dave, she'd never thought of him as any kind of threat.

Wanda knew Hank wasn't the kind to hurt anybody. He'd only hit her twice in the six years they'd been married and as soon as he'd done it he'd got down in the floor and apologized. Grabbed her and begged the same way she'd grabbed Dave the night before. He was just confused, she thought, getting an armful of wood from the pile Dave had made felling a tree.

He's harmless, she'd said to Dave after Hank had left one night. He'd been covered in blood, his two front teeth knocked out. He's lonely, she said.

190

He's out of his goddamn mind, Dave had said. Like a rabid dog that needs put down.

She stacked the wood in a triangle like Dave had showed her on their last camping trip and sprinkled some twigs and kindling at the base. She grabbed a lighter and some lighter fluid from under the charcoal grill out there and wet the wood and kindling. She sparked it with the lighter and before long the fire was picking up and growing higher.

When she came in Dave was standing in the doorway leading to the living room, stripped down to his boxers, his shirt and jeans slung over the back of one of the kitchen chairs. He had another beer in hand. Throw those clothes on, he said. I'm going to hop in the shower.

All right, Wanda said. She thought of some things to say and didn't say any of them.

And when you're done, he said, slide that shotgun into the closet.

In the space? she said. She thought he was talking about the space in the back of the wall they'd found a few months before. It had a small hidden door that blended into the rest of the wall. Dave had said that whoever built the house must've had something to hide.

In the space, Dave said and took a drink of the beer. Maybe tomorrow we'll go on a trip, he said.

Why would we go on a trip? she said. What about work?

I don't know, Dave said. Thinking about quitting. Thinking maybe we ought to go out and see what there is to see.

I'd like that, Wanda said. I think I'd really like to go

on a trip.

I was thinking about it, he said, still looking out into the living room. Wanda looked at him standing there, breathing. She looked at the map of hair that covered his shoulders and back and legs. You've never been on vacation, have you darling?

She hadn't. No, she said. Closest I've ever been was that trip we took to Holiday World.

That's what I thought, he said. Tell me, he said, where you want to go?

I don't know, honey, she said. I don't care where we go long as you love me.

Uh huh, he said.

And you love me, she said.

I love you, he said.

Good, she said. That's all I need.

Throw those clothes on, he said and tossed his half-empty beer into the living room. It hit something and she could hear it spilling out. I'm gonna get cleaned up. Then we need to pack.

He was gone then, walking in the direction of the bathroom, and she picked up the shirt and jeans he'd left on the kitchen chair and carried them into the backyard. The fire was going well at that point and when she tossed them on it quickly swallowed them and they were curling and burning in no time at all. She stood there watching until she was sure they would burn up all the way.

Back inside she grabbed his shotgun by the door and took it into their bedroom. At first she thought of how she needed to clean but then remembered they were going on vacation and it didn't matter. So she trudged through the mounds of clothes and sacks of things and opened the closet. The closet itself was crammed with more clothes and a couple of old TVs that didn't work anymore. There was also a backpack that Wanda had used for awhile when the truck had broken down and she'd had to walk to the store to buy groceries.

She looked at the backpack and thought of what was inside. There were some old shopping lists and notes she'd made to herself, but there were also some things she hid in there so Dave wouldn't find them. She unzipped it and filed through and came to the green folder she was looking for. In the folder were some letters Hank had given her back when they'd been married. They were letters that promised he'd be a better man and appreciate her more. They were letters that went on and on about how beautiful he thought she was and how he was going to spend the rest of his life trying to make her feel loved.

Those were all in one side of the folder and in the other pocket was a picture she'd taken of Hank once upon a time. It was from when he'd taken her to the state fair in Indianapolis. She hadn't wanted to go but he'd pushed and pushed until she'd finally agreed. In the end she was happy he'd convinced her. There'd been so many people there and so much food and music she'd felt dizzy with happiness.

The picture was of Hank in the livestock barn. They'd been looking at all the prize cows and goats and had seen this giant pig standing in a stall all by himself. He was fat and pink and snuffling through a mound of hay. Hank pulled her over and pointed at that pig.

That boy right there, he'd said to her, is gonna make a hell of a pan of bacon someday.

Wanda had laughed until she cried at that. Hank knew how to tickle her sometimes and he got to work touching her side and under her arms until she couldn't stop giggling. Then he'd thrown one of his legs over the gate to the stall and, in the same motion, handed her the disposable camera they'd brought for the occasion. Get a picture, he'd said, jumping in and running over to that pig. He squatted down and put his arm around it. Hurry up, he said to her as she fumbled with the camera, snap it fast.

She'd hit the button just as he shot her a grin. The picture made him look like a handsome farmer, what with his faded hat pulled down over his eyes and the pair of overalls he was always wearing.

Wanda looked at the picture and got to laughing all over again. Then she heard the shower shut off. She shoved the picture into the folder and then the folder into the backpack. She took the shotgun and the backpack and pushed them both into the space in the wall. She closed the panel behind them and thought about all the things she wouldn't need anymore.

✪ ABOUT THE AUTHOR ✪

Jared Yates Sexton is a born-and-bred Hoosier living and working in The South as an Assistant Professor of Creative Writing at Georgia Southern University. His work has appeared in publications around the world and his first short story collection, *An End To All Things*, is available from Atticus Books.

Split Lip Press

www.splitlippress.com

www.splitlipmagazine.com

www.facebook.com/splitlippress

www.twitter.com/splitlippress